DRAGON THIEF SERIES

SEASON ONE
Dragon Thief

The Chicago Job

The Poisons Book Job

The Vault Job

The Femme Fatale Job

The Scavenger Job

SEASON TWO
The Crown of Kingship Job

The Green Scroll Job

The Payback Job

THE CHICAGO JOB

A DRAGON THIEF STORY

DRAGON THIEF

BOOK TWO

KAT SIMONS

T&D
PUBLISHING

The Chicago Job

To my boys, because they're the best.
To my family, for everything.

ONE

Taking a stupid bet and breaking into the dragon king's hoard had been Myra's first mistake.

Thinking she'd be able to get away with doing just one job to make up for that lapse in judgement had been her second.

She was still deciding if kissing the dragon king's son had been the third mistake. Jury was still out. Depended on how this current confrontation went.

Standing in the middle of the dragon king's court, in an elaborate mansion some people might have called a castle, amidst a compound of other buildings, circled by a fortified wall, built among the hills and hard gray rock in the far upper west end of Manhattan, Myra had assumed she'd hand

Christopher over to his father, bid them both farewell, and that would be her done with the dragons. At least with the king. With Christopher…

Again, jury still out.

But the dragon king had decided to throw all those assumptions into the trash and make Myra rethink all her life choices. Or at least the one, very bad choice that had put pride before common sense when she took that bet.

She suspected the reason the king wasn't done with her yet was because she'd *succeeded* in breeching his hoard more than the fact that she'd attempted it. Lots of thieves eventually attempted to break into a dragon hoard. Hard to resist all that gold and jewelry and cash and bonds and…well, the wealth. The sheer wealth. Who could resist that?

But most thieves couldn't get around the security of a dragon hoard. Especially not a dragon king's hoard. They usually got caught somewhere along that process, still a long way from actually reaching the treasure.

Myra had gotten caught standing in the middle of the hoard admiring some of the crown jewels.

Fortunately for her, those skills were more valuable to the dragon king than killing her as an example would have been. And also fortunately—

maybe?—she'd broken in just after the king's son had gotten stolen. Yes, yes, technically Christopher insisted he'd been kidnapped, not stolen. But she was a thief. She stole things. She thought in terms of theft. Not kidnapping. Returning a stolen item was within her purview.

And that's what she'd done. Retrieved Christopher from the shapeshifters and wizard who'd stolen him, and then returned him to the king unharmed. Mostly.

True, she'd assumed she'd been sent in to rescue a kid—because the king kept calling his son a youngling—and her plan to get back out of the high-rise building had needed to be changed at the last minute. She was good at improvisation, though. And she'd had backup plans. Multiple backup plans.

Those plans just hadn't accounted for the near seven-foot-tall wall of muscle and adult male physique standing next to her.

Still, they'd gotten out alive and unsinged. Only the kidnappers had gotten burned. Myra considered that a job well done.

The king had decided that her completing this excellent bit of work was not quite enough.

"Father, you've asked enough of her. Let it go." Christopher shifted his position to stand just a little in front of her as they faced his father, which was nice because standing before a dragon king was intimidating as hell even if the king was in human and not dragon form at that moment.

Sitting on an elaborate throne made of bones and gold with some winking jewelry in between. She'd eyed that throne the first time she'd seen it, wondering how hard it would be to remove, say, that little diamond near the base without anyone noticing.

She had not been left alone for long enough to find out.

Like his son, the dragon king was a huge man, standing well over six and a half feet tall in human form, with dark black curly hair cut neatly, and light eyes that switched from blue to green depending on the light. His skin tone was pale in this form. She'd never personally seen him in dragon form, but the rumor was his scales were bronze colored, with a bit of red. She had no idea how old he was because dragon shifters aged different to humans, but he'd been around and been king for a long time, so she assumed he was old. There were silver threads in his dark hair, but it was hard to tell if those were natural or an affectation to give himself gravitas. With the king, you just couldn't be sure.

Unlike his son, the king was what one would call classically handsome. The bones on his face and jaw were strong, his features perfectly symmetrical, his forehead high under his crown, his lips thin but suited his facial structure. Had he wanted to, the king could have made a killing as a leading man in Hollywood. Probably wouldn't have even mattered if he could act. Because even outside of the good looks, he was compelling. There was a sort of aura to him that made people notice him. An inner power that took up space and commanded rooms.

He and Christopher shared that trait even if they didn't share much in the way of looks.

Probably helped they could both shift into dragons the size of low-rise buildings.

"She is not done with repaying me for my magnanimous decision not to kill her," the king said in answer to his son, his voice deep, rolling through the high ceiling room like thunder.

"She showed you exactly where your security systems were weak and vulnerable before anyone with real nefarious intent got in," Christopher said. "And she assisted me in breaking out of the tower so you couldn't be forced to do something…difficult to take back."

The shifters and wizard had been trying to get a relic the king kept in his hoard that, according to Christopher, turned shifters into unkillable monsters. That would have been bad. She'd been delighted not to have been the one committing that fuck up and handing the relic over. No one had even mentioned a relic to her. She'd taken a bet from an old rival, to prove she could get into the hoard. And all she'd intended on taking out was a trinket to prove she'd been there.

But, after hearing what Christopher had to say about his kidnappers, she realized she'd been the guinea pig, the one they'd sent in to see if it was even possible to get into the king's hoard. Her rival might have even been working with the shifters, though she'd have to question him to find out. Even if he hadn't, even if he'd been tricked into issuing her the bet, the end result had been her getting into the king's hoard, only to get caught.

Kidnapping Christopher was their insurance plan if the break in hadn't succeeded. Stealing the relic, or blackmailing the king with one of his son's lives…either way would get the job done.

No one expected the king to hire a thief to get Christopher back.

"One more job," the king said. "Nothing that isn't within your realm of expertise." He spoke directly to Myra, ignoring his son's comment. "And we will consider ourselves even."

"My debt was paid when I got Christopher back," she said. "You want me to do a job for you now, that'll require payment. Up front. And details before I accept."

She was bluffing. Big time.

First, she never worked for other people. No one hired her to steal things. She stole because she wanted to. What she wanted to. When she wanted to.

But in reality, if the dragon king told you to do a job for him, there wasn't an awful lot someone like her could do about it. Except turn it down and then die. She didn't want to die, so she'd accept the job. So long as it didn't involve doing something she didn't do. Like kill people.

The king's expression tightened but that was his only show of tension. A blink and he smiled at her. It was not a comforting smile. There were a lot of teeth involved. Reminding her that in his other form, the king could swallow her whole.

"There's a relic that has long eluded me. But it would be infinitely safer inside my hoard rather than loose for any…any unscrupulous individual to access."

"What's this relic do?" She'd been left in the dark about the monster creating relic last time. She didn't want to make that same mistake.

"Nothing humans need worry about."

She came within a microsecond of snort-laughing at that comment. With all the dragons around Manhattan, a human with any sense in their head always worried about the things those dragons did or were interested in. Just common sense in this world. The dragons might go out of their way not to appear as dragons very often. And they usually cloaked when flying around for the comfort and peace of mind of humans. But that didn't keep humans from worrying about what the dragons did.

Instead of laughing, she gave the king a very level look. She couldn't completely ignore the unfortunate tingle of curiosity that moved through her blood, though.

"What's the relic?" she said.

She wasn't saying she'd actually take the job. But she wasn't saying she wouldn't either. In fact, even though working for the dragon king was a bad idea and she didn't consider she owed him anything else anymore—she *had* just brought him back his son alive and well—her own curiosity did tend to get the better of her.

Between her curiosity and her professional pride lay the seeds of her own destruction.

But what could a thief do.

Two

The king considered Myra from his bejeweled bone and gold throne. The chill in the high-ceilinged throne room seemed to get momentarily chillier. The scent of dragon—a mix of reptile and sulfur but with a hint of leather—got a bit stronger.

Myra ignored the faint warning signals and waited him out. If he wanted her to do a job for him, she did have to know what she was going to be stealing.

A moment passed in that chilly silence. A beat. And then, "The relic is a chalice. A goblet." The king smiled.

Or really it was a stretching of his mouth into the semblance of a smile. This was another place where he and his son diverged. She found

Christopher's smile charming. The king's was terrifying.

"Chalice? A cup. Is it made of precious stones and gold?" Because that would encourage her to take this job. She liked precious stones and gold.

"No."

Too bad.

"It's made of something more valuable."

"Something more valuable than precious stones and gold?" She shook her head. "Platinum?"

This made the king chuckle. "It's made of the skin and bones of a dragon."

"That sounds…kinda gross." A cup made of skin and bone? Not. Good. "Cursed, is it?"

It had to be a curse, right. No one made things from skin and bone that didn't have magic and curses involved, and she was not a magic and curses kind of person.

Well, that wasn't entirely true. She was a magic person. Her magic just ran toward skills that made breaking and entering easy, like an ability to hide her scent and some magic lock-picking skills. And she liked stealing a certain caliber of magical item because they brought a good price. She drew the line, though, at magically cursed things that required skin and bone to make them.

"Not so much cursed as bespelled with power that is too deadly to be loose in the world."

"Then why is it loose in the world? Out of curiosity."

"This isn't something a human should be sent to retrieve," Christopher said before the king could answer.

"Didn't say I was going to go get it yet," she pointed out to him.

He didn't glance down at her. Which was annoying. And maybe stung a little. If she allowed herself to notice the sensation.

The king kept his assessing gaze on her, though. Not glancing at his son. If the king's gaze wasn't so damned intimidating, that might have given her an ounce of smugness. *Someone* wasn't afraid to look at her in front of his relatives.

"I think, given what our Myra is capable of, she is the perfect one to retrieve the chalice."

Our Myra?

"I'm not a dragon," she said. "Not a subject of your majesty's." That had to be very clear right here and now or she was a little afraid she'd somehow end up a subject of the king's without noticing. Something about him and the way he wielded power…implied that.

"But we both know you'll do this for me," the king said.

"Oh? Do we?"

"I pay well."

"That would help. Except I don't normally work for others."

"For this amount of money, I'm sure you'll make an exception."

"I don't just work for the money, either."

And that was true. It was also what got her into trouble more often than the money. The money was good. But not the real challenge. The real challenge was *could she get away with it.* Could she do the thing that no one else could do. That was the fun part.

"The chalice is kept in a vault. It shouldn't be an issue for you."

"Then why would I bother?"

"Because getting *to* the vault is impossible."

"Nothing's impossible." Just very difficult. Unfortunately, though, the king had her now. He'd hit his mark with that shot. She loved very difficult. Still, wouldn't do to let him know too soon how interested she was. "Describe impossible, just so we're clear."

"The vault itself is inside a building owned by a wizard. A multi-story complex with several subterranean levels. It fronts as a business bank and financial institution, but no one enters or leaves without permission. The building is bespelled so that only invited guests can get past the entryway. Anyone else who tries…dissolves.”

“Fun.”

“Father,” Christopher barked. “She’s not taking this job.”

“I can speak for myself.” Myra didn’t take her gaze off the king to glance at Christopher this time. “Go on.”

“If, and that’s a rare if, someone manages to get past the initial security spell, the entire compound is rigged with traps—both physical and magical—that change on a regular basis. The elevators, maintenance shafts, even some of the floors are all set with traps.”

“What level is the vault on?”

“In the very center of the building, on the second subterranean level. There are two more levels beneath the vault floor. Both are also bespelled with traps.”

“Of course they are. And obviously no window access to the level with the vault.”

“Or tunnel access. The ground beneath the building is also bespelled. As are the walls that make up the building.”

“In the city?”

“In *a* city,” the king said.

“Where?”

“Father,” Christopher said again. “No.”

Both Myra and the king ignored Christopher's growl. "Chicago," the king said.

Ah. There was the rub. "Chicago is inside another dragon's kingdom. Is that why you haven't gone after the chalice?"

"There are…treaties."

"So no dragons can go after this cup?"

"Not officially. No." His gaze danced to his son and away so fast she might have missed the gesture if she hadn't been watching him so closely. And wasn't that glance interesting.

"Why's it not just as safe in the wizard's vault as it would be inside your hoard. Sounds impossible to get at." For some people. "Why not just leave it there if it's been there for a while already not causing any mischief?"

"It is not safer with the wizard," the king said, his expression going cold and stoney. "It belongs with the dragons."

"Then why doesn't the Chicago king go after it? It's in his territory."

"He is too busy attempting to quell a rebellion among his dragons to deal with the situation. I would, in fact, be doing him a favor by retrieving the relic."

"Sure." That's what the king would be doing. Right. "This rebellion… That going to cause any issues with the heist. *If* I agree to go after this chalice," she added just to be clear.

"Shouldn't."

The king was lying to her. But he'd also presented her with an impossible job, something she had a very hard time resisting. "What else don't I know? If I touch the chalice, will I die? Turn into a dragon? A monster?"

"Touching it… No. Drinking from it would be bad, though."

"Good to know." Shouldn't be too hard to avoid drinking from a skin and bone cup. The very idea made her own skin crawl.

"You can't send her into enemy territory like this," Christopher said. "She's not a dragon."

The king flicked a glance at his son this time, his smile deepening. A disturbing smile, that. "No. She's not. Which is why I can send her in without risking a war."

"She can't go alone."

Now the king directed his full attention on Christopher. "Are you volunteering?"

Her turn to look up at Christopher. Was he volunteering?

"She can't go alone. The territory, and the relic, are too dangerous."

"I work alone just fine," she said.

"I'll go." This said to his father, ignoring her comment.

That wasn't something she'd tolerate for long, sexy shoulders and impressive height be damned.

"The son of the king can't be caught," the king said. "This time."

Oh. That was a dig. And not a very nice one either. She saw the comment hit home, but only in the way Christopher's jaw tightened slightly before returning to its normal state of rock hard and intractable.

"I'm going," Christopher said. "We'll stay below the radar."

"I haven't agreed to the job yet," she pointed out.

"But you're going to," the king said. "It's a challenge."

Bastard. "What are you paying me?" If he was going to have her number, she was going to get paid well for it.

He named enough money—cash and gold—to set her up for the next few years. Not that she wasn't already sufficiently set up. But the amount of money on offer was obscene. Easily four times what she normally made on a job.

If he was willing to offer that much in payment, it meant the relic was worth easily five times that amount. If not more. Might even be a priceless artifact.

She'd only swiped a few priceless things in her life. Okay, maybe a few more than a few, but still. Not as many priceless things as things with very definitive prices.

She nodded slowly at the king. "Money in my account before I start."

"How do I know you'll complete the task and not just run off with my money?"

She lowered her chin and gave him a look. "I'm a thief. Not a liar. I have my reputation to protect."

"An impressive reputation at that."

"Consider it a good faith gesture," she said.

"You broke into my hoard. I don't have *good* faith in you."

She grinned. "But you have faith in my skills or we wouldn't be talking."

"You will take my son. He will ensure you live. Or if you don't, that I can get my money back after you die."

Christopher growled, a sound so quiet it was hard for her human ears to even pick up. But she was certain his father heard. And there was an odd sort of hissing in that growl. A combination of sounds a human couldn't make.

"Fair," she said to the king. "I usually work

alone. But with dragon politics a possible issue, I'll allow it. This time."

Except the son of one king getting caught in another king's territory during a time of rebellion would create *more* of a political problem than just her sneaking in.

She wasn't entirely sure why she was agreeing to take Christopher with her on this job. Why she was agreeing to the *job*. The Christopher part… That probably had something to do with the kiss. And whether or not it had been a mistake.

The job…

Well. She never could resist a challenge.

She glanced up at Christopher and smiled, wagging her brows. "This could be fun."

THREE

"This is a damsel in distress thing, isn't it?" Myra asked Christopher as they stepped out onto the roof of the mansion that looked more like a castle.

No exiting through the front door like a normal human for the dragon shifters. Even if she hadn't come with Christopher flying her in, she'd have had to have been flown in by some other dragon to be allowed entrance to the mansion.

Not that there wasn't a main door entrance, but anyone who came there got greeted by one of the king's staff and never got farther. You wanted an audience with the king, you flew in. And it helped if you had an appointment.

If you didn't want to see the king, and were just looking to break into the king's hoard, you took a different route all together and avoided the front door and the roof at all costs.

The king had done up the roof, a long flat space that spanned the length of the huge house, lining the low wall encircling the building with dragon statues and carpeting one half of the stone roof with grass—real grass somehow—so the younglings had a softer landing. The other half was covered in smooth red sandstone that matched the rest of the building. There were two actual, honest-to-god guard towers at either end of the mansion—which was one of the elements that made it looked like a castle—from which dragon sentries ensured those approaching were welcome.

Myra hadn't directly seen how those guards dealt with unauthorized approaches on the mansion, but the rumors said it involved streams of fire and charred remains and really that was all she needed to know.

Thick woods covered the rocky hill on which the mansion and the surrounding compound sat, and beyond those, a long road met up with the main streets of Manhattan. From up here, she could see the lights and sparkle of the city spreading out below, and far off on the horizon to the east, a pink line across the sky signaled the approaching sunrise.

She'd basically been up all night, first rescuing

Christopher, then returning him here. But the buzz of the evening still sang in her blood, leaving her more restless than tired. She'd be tired in an hour when the adrenaline from the last few minutes wore off.

Christopher, also staring out over the city in the distance, didn't respond to her dig, so she bumped his bare arm with her shoulder and got him to look down at her. He'd taken a brief minute to change after they'd arrived, before they had the audience with his father, but he hadn't changed much. He still had no shirt on, only a new set of clean, unripped, black dress pants. He'd also remained barefoot. Barefoot looked very cold on the stone roof.

The autumn was progressing. The trees spreading out below them were a multi-colored patchwork of oranges, reds, yellows mixed with evergreens. But that beauty would fade soon. Winter wasn't that far off.

When Christopher—not Chris, she'd learned last night—met her gaze, she grinned. "This isn't me being a damsel in distress," she assured him. "You don't have to come with me to steal back the chalice."

"I'm coming with you." His voice was still deep and his mood was hard to read. "It's not a damsel in distress thing," he finished, looking a little uncomfortable.

And entirely too sexy and adorable. That was his soft spot, apparently. Damsels in distress. She loved that about him. It had gotten him into trouble, at least once that she knew of. The other dragons saw it as a weakness. But she thought it was sweet.

She nodded and looked out over the city again, feeling his wings spread out behind her. He could shift just that much of him, opening wings while the rest of his body stayed in human form. She'd had no idea dragon shifters could do that before last night. Turned out she knew very little about the dragons. Just that she mostly tried to avoid them.

At present, she was doing a piss-poor job of avoiding them.

"I need to sleep and do a little planning before we leave," she said as she turned and jumped up into his arms, delighted when he caught her without comment or hesitation. A little tingling started low in her stomach. He was very warm. Almost hot. The scales over his shoulders and chest soft and pliant under her sensitive fingertips. Last night, she'd sworn he smelled like sugar cookies. A funny sort of scent for a dragon shifter. This morning, she picked up more of the leather and musk smell of dragons she'd gotten from inside the mansion.

"Drop me off somewhere close to a subway station," she said, trying not to run her fingers over his shoulders.

He scowled. "I should take you home."

"Is that a proposition?" she asked, waggling her eyebrows.

His scowl deepened, but something hot and knowing moved through his gaze, increasing those tingles in her stomach. His arms flexed against her, where one curled around her back and the other under her knees. Like this, she was almost nose to nose with him, which made watching the changing emotions in his expression very easy, and super fascinating.

"I meant, I would feel better not just leaving you on a city street."

"I'll be fine, big guy. I'm capable of getting myself home. I'm capable of getting myself almost anywhere." Which was what had gotten her into all this in the first place.

"Fine. Where and when will we meet later."

"Tomorrow—" He opened his mouth and she held up a hand. "I need time to plan and research." That was her excuse anyway. She already had most of a plan. She just needed to work out the details. "The chalice isn't going anywhere and if it does, I'll learn about it during my research. Plus, I need sleep. Remember?"

He grunted, snapped his wings out to the side, and stepped up onto the low wall circling the roof. She looked down to the heavily tree-filled ground far below. Lot of hard rocks down there. She met Christopher's gaze. He met hers. Then he stepped off the side of the building.

Her stomach tumbled in the moments of freefall before the first downbeat of his wings caught an air current and dragged them back upward again.

She grinned. "That's fun."

His answering grunt made her chuckle.

He circled back toward the city, taking them beyond his father's estate and out over the edges of neighborhood houses and low-rise buildings, farther into the city than she'd expected him to take her. Moving over higher apartment complexes and neighborhood parks, streets lined with restaurants and bodegas just opening their doors to welcome the morning commuters. Her stomach growled at the thought of a bagel and coffee, which earned her a raised brow from Christopher.

She shrugged. "Been an adventurous night. I need to eat."

"So do I," he admitted.

Myra hadn't expected such a simple comment to be so full of innuendo but there it was. Hanging in the air around them. Making those tingles in her stomach start up again. She ignored them because, for the moment, they had to work together and the implications of that earlier kiss were going to have to wait.

"You'll be free of me soon and can get yourself fed. Don't go rescuing any distressed damsels before tomorrow, though. I can't be rescuing you every day."

That earned her another grumpier sounding grunt.

He landed lightly at the edge of the Colombia University campus, touching down on the sidewalk and folding his wings back in the same move. He didn't immediately set her down, but searched their surroundings first, as if looking out for danger.

Myra had to press her lips together not to grin again. He was ridiculously gallant.

She gave his chest a pat and he set her back on her feet, dropping his hold under her knees first and keeping a hand at her back until she was on the sidewalk. Even then, it took him one longer beat than necessary before he dropped his hold.

More stomach tingles. "I'm good from here. Meet me tomorrow at noon at Penn."

"I can fly us to Chicago."

"First, too cold." Dragon flight through the city was cold enough. He was so warm, his skin pumping off heat like a furnace, he kept her from freezing while they flew, but still. "Second, too obvious. Even if you cloak. We're going into a rival king's territory. No point in alerting them to us ahead of time. And third, I like the train."

"We're taking a train?"

He sounded so horrified, she grinned. "Can't take a commercial airline. Too much security to get through, and I'm going to need a few things I'd rather not have to check."

"That's a twenty-four-hour train ride," he said.

"Yup." She gave him another pat on his bare chest, which was unnecessary to their upcoming job but was good for her mood. "Pack light. We won't be able to hang out in Chicago long."

Mores the pity. She liked Chicago and hadn't been there in a few years. Be nice to see more of the place. Wouldn't hurt her feelings to take in the city with the handsome man beside her either. Although, handsome wasn't quite the right word for Christopher. Not like his father. Christopher was…compelling. Hard not to look at—she imagined even with a shirt on he'd be hard to ignore. Something about the arrangement of features, his piercing blue eyes, the hard line of his jaw. Taken individually, his features shouldn't have worked together, but his did, and the overall effect was magnetic.

"I could just fly us there," he repeated, his brows raised.

"Too cold," she also repeated. "Too long a flight." Unless dragon shifters could rearrange space-time during long flights? She had no idea.

She really really had to learn more about dragon shifters. She knew the bare minimum, like everyone else. Just enough to know to avoid them and to stay on their good sides if encountering them. She probably needed to ask Christopher more questions about what he could and couldn't do.

Which was another good reason for the long train ride.

"I could keep you warm while in flight," he said, his voice deepening.

And the innuendo there made her head spin. Yeah he could.

Wait, that wasn't what they were supposed to be talking about. "I'm still not up for a multi-hour dragon flight."

Although, maybe one day. Because actually, dragon flight was pretty fun. When you got over the fact that you were looking at the city from a very unique angle. She wasn't afraid of heights, but even she'd had to take a moment to adjust to that new view.

"We're going by train," she said, firmly, to put an end to the discussion. Because anymore innuendo would derail her intention to get some research on the chalice done before they left. "We're going into territory where you shouldn't be. That means going in in a way that won't be obvious. Dragon flight is obvious. People tend to notice the wings."

"You'd be surprised what people *don't* notice."

Actually, she often was. "My point is still valid. Just in case, we go in the way humans would, and we try to ensure no one notices one of the dragon king's sons is in another dragon king's territory until after we're well gone. It'll be enough having to deal with another wizard."

While she had magical skills herself—all aligned with her occupation as thief—she didn't spend a lot of time around other magical people. And she avoided wizards when she could. Bastards were a pain in the ass. Her latest encounter with one, just last night, had nearly gotten her killed. Having to deal with another one so soon had her especially cautious. Which was a new feeling for her. Caution wasn't usually her strong suit.

"Tomorrow at noon," she said. "Penn Station. Main Amtrak hall."

"It's a big station. We need a more specific location."

She looked him over. "Christopher. You are hard to miss." She was tempted to pat his bare arm, but she thought better of it. Too distracting. "Don't worry. I'll spot you. Just be there on time. I don't want to miss the train."

"How do you already know what time the train to Chicago leaves?"

She grinned. "Go get some shoes on. You're making me cold looking at you."

He held her gaze for a long moment, like he intended on continuing the argument over the train. Or maybe exploring the innuendo a little more. That thought had those tingles in her stomach dancing again. Actually, she was pretty sure they'd never stopped.

Her gaze dropped to his mouth as she waited for him to speak. And the memory of what his lips had felt like against hers had her breathing a little unsteady.

But after a beat, a moment filled with all kinds of potential, he simply said, "Get home safe so I don't have to come rescue you again."

"I rescued you."

"And then I had to rescue you."

"So we're even then."

He chuckled. It was a very sexy chuckle.

"See you tomorrow, your highness," she said, and enjoyed his scowl. "Get some rest. You've had a rough week."

"And you? You'll rest?"

She didn't need rest. She had a heist to plan.

Four

Myra didn't answer any of Christopher's questions until they were settled onto the train in their sleeper car. She'd arranged the private bedroom suite, using some of the money the dragon king had given her upfront to pay for the job. Had she been traveling alone, she'd have booked a roomette, or maybe even a coach seat and just slept sitting up. She could afford the sleeper car. She just preferred the ability to keep an eye on her surroundings that a coach seat afforded.

Plus, never knew when an opportunity might arise from an overheard conversation or chance meeting. Couldn't have those lucky bits of serendipity as easily from inside a private room.

But she and Christopher were going to need

privacy to talk about the upcoming job. And honestly, he was so hard to miss in a crowd, being as he stood a foot taller than the average human, it was better to have him tucked away in a private space where he drew less attention. They were attempting to reach Chicago inconspicuously.

She'd splurged on the suite rather than gotten them separate rooms because the dragon king was paying and because it would make talking easier. But even in the relative luxury of having individual room spaces separated by individual, tiny bathrooms and a narrow corridor, the suite was still pretty small. Especially when her roommate was so large. When standing, Christopher had to duck to keep from bashing his head on the ceiling. And she wasn't entirely sure the fold down beds were going to hold him. He'd definitely have a hard time stretching out. Wasn't much she could do about that. There was only so much room on a train.

The tight confines were going to test her professionalism, though.

He settled on the long couch, that would eventually turn into a bed. She sat in one of the fold-down chairs that gave her a good view out the window and put as much space between her and Christopher as the room allowed. Still, bumping knees was entirely too easy as the train jerked into motion.

"So what did you learn?" he asked, his gaze darting out the window to the platform as the train moved out of the station, slowly chunking along the tracks.

"I learned that your father is a terrible liar," she said.

His brows rose, but that was the extent of his reaction.

"The rebellion in the Chicago king's territory is more significant and much more likely to cause us issues since some of the rebellious dragons are working with the wizard holding this chalice I'm supposed to steal."

Christopher's brows lowered dangerously. "I was not made aware of that part."

"Didn't think you were or you would have mentioned it."

She wasn't sure why she thought he would be honest with her where his father hadn't been. She barely knew the man. But there was a sense of honor there that spoke to his honesty. A degree of chivalry she rarely encountered these days, chivalry that wouldn't allow him to lie to her about potential dangers.

Plus, he was only coming along on this caper because he assumed she needed help and he couldn't resist helping a damsel in distress. Not that she was particularly distressed about anything she'd learned. Most of it just upped the challenge of this job.

"But I was pretty sure the way your father tried to downplay the rebellion that it was going to cause us trouble. And I was right. We'll have to go around both dragon shifters *and* the wizard's spells to get through the building."

"And how do you intend on doing that?"

She grinned. "Remember when we met and you couldn't pick up my scent?"

He grunted, a reply she took as a yes.

"I've got a spell for that." She waggled her fingers at him. "That'll take care of the dragons' ability to smell us. All you shifters rely on your heightened senses too much. It's a weakness."

Another eyebrow raise. This one sardonic.

"As for the ever-changing spells inside the building, that's a little trickier."

"Do you have a spell for that?"

"Don't need one. I double checked your father's information, because he's an untrustworthy source, but it turns out he was right about the level of magical difficulty involved. Spells all over the building, popping up in random places, designed to kill or liquify or cause any manner of disgusting damage. There's no predictable pattern to the spells or where they'll show up. They are constantly cycling around the entire building, including in the usual thief places like air ducts and elevator shafts."

His half smile got those tingles in her stomach going again. That was going to be very distracting. She should probably ask him to stop smiling like that at her.

"I remember your fondness for air ducts and elevator shafts. Also climbing along ledges outside buildings," he said.

"It's a cat burglar thing." She shrugged. "At any rate, the randomness and severity of the spells ensures no one who doesn't belong can move through the building without risking a horrible, painful death."

"As my father said."

"Ah, but see, here's the thing. There are people who *belong* in the building. People work there and have to move around despite all the spells scattered everywhere. And you can't have your employees and henchmen getting themselves killed regularly because of all the spells popping on and off around the place, changing constantly, now can you?"

He frowned, leaning forward slightly. That closed the space between them in the tight cabin, which did nothing for those tingles in her stomach. "So there must be something that keeps the people allowed in the building from being affected by the spells."

"Exactly."

"Another spell? A preventative shield?"

"An employee ID card."

He blinked. "An ID card? An ordinary ID card?"

"Okay, a bespelled ID card. But yeah, a card."

"How does that work?"

"The ID card is…tagged, I guess you'd call it. There's a magical microchip inside that the death spells recognize. If you've got one of these cards on you, the spells recognize you as someone who belongs in the building, and they don't explode you. Without an ID card, you die."

"You talk about dying very casually."

"Oh, I'm not casual about my own death. I have no intention of getting liquified by a wizard spell. Just relaying facts about the situation here."

He leaned back again. "But if all it takes is someone *carrying* a physical object like a card around in their pocket, can't an employee just… hand their own ID to another person and give them access to the building? Or couldn't a thief like you just steal one? Is that your plan?"

"Wouldn't that be entirely too easy. No. And

I'm insulted you'd think I'd do a job that was as simple as picking a pocket."

He pressed his lips together, leaving her wondering if he was annoyed or trying not to laugh. Based on the look in his eyes, she was going to go with laugh.

"No, each ID is coded to an individual's DNA. The DNA signature is linked with the magical microchips spell. The card can't actually be handled by another person without the card melting."

"So…someone's spouse moving the card to dust would be bad?"

"Very, if said someone wants to remain employed at the wizard's place. Motivates everyone to take very very good care of their ID cards, as well. No randomly forgetting your card in the bathroom or dropping it on the 'L', right?"

"Probably saves a lot of money having to replace lost cards," he said.

"Definitely." She glanced out the window as they moved above ground, chugging along the west side of Manhattan, with spectacular views out the left side of the train of the Hudson River. If they could see out of the right side of the train, she suspected they'd be able to see the dragon king's mansion, or at least some of it in passing. But their suite's view looked across the river to New Jersey instead. She didn't mind. The river view was soothing.

"So you can't just steal someone's ID card?" Christopher said, bringing her back to their conversation. "How do these cards help us get into the building?"

"Actually, you're going to be more complicated to get in than I will be. Seems the dragons that work with the wizard need very specific cards. Dragon DNA being a different animal, so to speak, from human DNA. There aren't very many of those. The wizard only lets so many dragons into his stronghold."

"Smart. Too many dragons and it'll become a dragon stronghold instead of the wizard's."

She had no doubt. "I'm still working out how to get you into the building. But I've got a card for myself already."

His brows snapped down and his mouth dropped open and it was the most satisfying thing she'd ever experienced, being able to shock the son of the dragon king. Well, maybe not *the* most satisfying experience. But it ranked right up there.

"How?" he demanded.

"Cleaning staff. Have to get around too. They were hiring."

"You got a job on the cleaning staff in less than twenty-four hours applying from New York?"

"I didn't say I applied and got hired. At least not in the technical sense." But she had hacked into the hiring agency's computer and inserted herself as a new hire. "I'll need to stop at HR to get my ID card coded to my DNA, but once that's done, I'm in. You will be another issue. I can't pass a dragon shifter off as cleaning crew. Especially because we have to worry about the dragons inside recognizing you as one of the New York king's sons."

He grunted at that reality. "I'm not letting you go in alone. We need to find me an ID card."

"Working on it as we speak."

"How?"

"Secret thief magic."

He dropped his chin and gave her a look.

She laughed. "Fine. My hacking skills are only so good, but good enough to run a scan of the dragon IDs on record. I'm looking for a match for your general physical appearance. Once I've got a candidate, we'll just need to arrange for his card to melt and you can step into HR to get a new one. They'll be using your DNA to the new card, so you'll be free to move around. So long as you avoid the other dragons who will know you are not who you claim to be."

"What if the dragon I'm pretending to be gets

to HR before we do? Or they discover the mistake while we're still inside."

"Got a plan for that, too. But it's still a little ephemeral. I'll get it worked out before we arrive."

"You'll get it worked out?"

"Yes. I will. Don't worry."

"Would it hurt your feelings if I said I was worried?"

"My professional pride, yes."

"Then I won't say it."

She tried not to get too soft inside over the fact that he didn't want to hurt her feelings, because he *had* insulted her professional skills. But since he didn't know how good she was at what she did, she'd forgive him this time.

"Don't worry," she repeated. "I've got it all worked out."

"Including where the chalice is inside the building?"

"Including that. Getting to it…"

Well, that, of course, was trickier.

FIVE

Dinner in the dining car was pleasant enough, and gave Myra a chance to study some of her fellow passengers. As she'd worried and suspected, though, Christopher drew an inordinate amount of attention.

He was hard not to look at, even though he was dressed casually in jeans and a long-sleeved dress shirt. He even wore shoes, which she appreciated—she was starting to notice he didn't like having shoes on all that much. His hair needed a cut, but he'd combed it. And nothing about his appearance superficially should have drawn attention. At least when he was sitting down.

But a man nearly seven-foot-tall walking

through a train car just drew attention. And it only took one look at his piercing blue eyes to startle the unwary. She was wary and his eyes sometimes still startled her.

She was also very aware of the whispers surrounding them. Her hearing wasn't as good as his, but that didn't keep her from picking up the spreading rumors, first as they'd entered the dining car and then after they'd been seated. The speculations started with wondering if he was a professional basketball player or a shapeshifter. No one could find pictures of him, so everyone in the dining card was convinced he was a shapeshifter.

And that was getting a little too close to home.

"It's probably not good that people are suspicious of you being a shifter," she whispered, leaning over, resting her forearms on the wood and Formica-covered table.

She raised her brows when she realized his ears moved, just a slight shift forward, but still. Human ears didn't move on the skull like that.

"It's only a few of them," he said, keeping his voice low too. "And most aren't assuming dragon."

"But a few are," she said.

He shrugged. "They've almost rejected the

idea, though. Why would a dragon be on a train and not flying, or even on a private jet?"

"Do you have a private jet?"

He lowered his chin and gave her a look. "Why would I need one?"

"I don't know… Fly your lovers around the world? Rescue damsels in distress in foreign countries? Take human associates partying? I have no idea what you do when you're not being kidnapped or helping me swipe a dangerous chalice."

And, she realized, she'd like to know more. She *wanted* to know what he did when he wasn't rescuing damsels. Her personal curiosity needed to wait until they weren't be watched by curious train passengers, but it didn't stop the questions nudging at her.

"I don't have a private jet," he said, after considering her for a silent moment. "Bad for the environment."

Her mouth twitched. She lost the battled not to chuckle. Then shook her head. "Environmentally conscious and likes to rescue damsels? What sort of dragon prince are you?" This last she said very quietly so no one else would hear them over the sounds of the train. She wasn't even sure he would until he answered her.

"The good kind."

Yeah. She sort of thought he was. Even if she didn't know what he spent his time doing most days.

They were served a remarkably yummy meal of steak and roasted vegetables. She indulged in the chocolate mousse dessert, which Christopher waved away.

"No chocolate?"

"I'm not crazy about chocolate."

She blinked. "Your first real flaw."

He gave her that raised eyebrow look that made her grin.

"More chocolate for me, then." She loved the stuff.

When they left the dining car, a few more whispers followed them. She listened close to pick up what she could, but once they were back in their sleeper car, she asked Christopher what he'd overheard with his superior hearing.

"I thought we shifters relied on our heightened senses too much," he said.

"You do. Doesn't mean I won't call on those heightened senses if we need them. What was everyone saying?"

"Most of it just gossip and nonsense. A few of the people who thought I might be a dragon shifter came back to that idea. Others were whispering that maybe I was famous and you were my… current relationship."

"Very careful about the way you said that." The whisperers had not been so discrete with their word choice.

That they didn't know who Christopher was, but were assuming he was *someone*, was a little difficult. She was very used to flying under the radar, so to speak, pun intended. Standing out in a crowd when she wasn't trying to was not a very comfortable feeling.

"The ones suspicious that you were a dragon shifter… What did they say specifically?"

He shrugged. "They were wondering if some of the stories about dragon shifters they'd read in the gossip rags might be about me. Someone suggested I looked familiar."

She'd heard that part. "Did you recognize them?"

"No. And there are no pictures of me online or in the press. They're confusing me with another dragon."

"So, the Hells Kitchen party…?" She kept her lips tight together so she wouldn't grin.

Even she'd heard about that party, which had turned into the social event of the year. And had devolved into absolute chaos. She didn't know Christopher very well. Maybe he was a party animal in his off time. But if he was, he did a good job of hiding that character trait. If he'd been involved in the Hells Kitchen event, it would be a very interesting insight into his character.

"Wasn't there," he said, his expression neutral. "Someone else was responsible for that."

"And the European prince?" She knew for a fact that rumor was about another, much more public facing dragon who performed on Broadway and didn't look anything like Christopher, but she was enjoying teasing Christopher.

"Never happened."

His deadpan response broke her grin free. "Not into princes? Just princesses?"

"There might have been the occasional prince in my past. Just not that one."

She chuckled, delighted with him and a little embarrassed by how charmed she was. "So none of the whispered rumors were about you?"

"None of those, no. Don't worry, most humans don't know who I am."

But they were getting a little too close to the truth. She was glad she'd gotten them a private suite now. The less they walked around among the other passengers, the better.

The fact that so many people knew all those rumors about various dragon shifters was a revelation, though. She'd spent most of her career avoiding dragon shifters and anything to do with them. Until the ill-fated bet and sneaking into the dragon king's hoard, she'd never attempted to steal from dragon shifters because she'd felt like that was courting trouble she didn't need. There were plenty of other people to steal from. Lots of wealthy people that didn't even miss their possessions. Didn't even know what they had because they had so much! She hadn't needed to tread on dragon toes to keep herself occupied over the years.

Obviously, that had given her a blind spot. A more serious one than she'd suspected.

"I really need to learn more about dragon shifters," she murmured, half to herself.

"Yes," Christopher said, his voice deep. "You do."

Something in his expression left her breathless, her pulse suddenly pounding in her throat. And those butterflies in her stomach were back. The shift in the air in the small room made her very aware once more of the fact that, although they had two different rooms and that little corridor and those two tiny bathrooms between where they'd be sleeping, the short distance wasn't much of a barrier.

A memory of their brief kiss the night she'd rescued him—and he'd rescued her in turn—made her lips tingle. It had been a very good kiss. She'd like to revisit that kiss.

But did she dare while they were supposed to be on a job?

The way Christopher's gaze dropped to her mouth she had a feeling he was thinking along similar lines. Neither of them moved for a long moment. Tension and anticipation danced along her nerves. They did have a whole night ahead of them.

But at the end, when the train reached Chicago, they had a job to do. One that was already dangerous. And he already had trouble resisting a woman in danger. If something happened between them tonight, would that make it harder for him to concentrate during the job?

Would it make it harder for *her* to concentrate?

Possible. Very possible.

They'd have time after the job. She hoped. She did want to explore these tingles more. And really wanted to revisit that kiss.

But maybe it was better if they didn't tonight.

"We need to sleep," she said, appalled to hear how disappointed she sounded. Not obvious at all, Myra. She rolled her eyes and huffed out a breath. Which made Christopher smile. The smile did not help.

"You gonna be able to sleep in that bunk?" she

asked, nodding to the fold down couch and, above it, the fold down bed.

"I can sleep anywhere," he said.

"Hey, me too." Well. They at least had something in common. Even if he didn't like chocolate.

She shuffled to her side of the suite and pulled down the top bunk.

"Not sleeping on the bottom?" Christopher said. His voice traveling across the small corridor that wasn't much of a corridor sounded intimate in the small space.

"I like the high ground," she said, glancing back. He'd pulled down the top bunk too, leaving the bottom as a couch.

"Me too," he said with a shrug.

He toed off his shoes, which she was a bit surprised he hadn't done the moment they walked into the room, and then disappeared into the tiny cubicle that was his bathroom. She shook her head. His shoulders would be bumping the wall in there, but they hadn't had a lot of choices.

She pulled off her own soft-soled black tennis shoes, leaving on her socks, and set her shoes near the door. They were slip-ons, easy to get into in the dark in an instant if needs be. The rest of her clothes—black leggings and a black cotton tunic—she kept on. The tunic looked nice enough to wear to dinner with a dragon prince but was comfortable enough to sleep in and conveniently meant she remained dressed overnight. She hung her multi-pocketed vest next to the door on a little coat latch, so she could grab that if she had to leave the room in a hurry. She'd packed the vest specifically for this trip, and all her good tools were hidden away in various pockets, including her best set of lockpicks. Because a woman never knew what she might need.

When Christopher came out of his tiny cubicle bathroom, she went into hers. Her nose twitched. The cubicle was very clean, and smelled strongly of the cleaning agent. She was grateful she didn't have a shifter sense of smell, though she wondered if the strong chemically scent bothered Christopher. By the time she came out, she half expected him to be up in his bunk already, but he was standing at the window, looking at the dark countryside. Not much to see, at least for her human eyes. Mostly darkness and trees, going by too fast to be more than a blur.

"You okay?" she asked, standing in the tiny space that passed for a corridor between their halves of the suite.

He didn't turn, but she could see him looking at her in the reflection on the dark window glass.

"I'd be better if my father hadn't asked you to do this."

"You do realize I wouldn't be doing this if I didn't want to, right?"

"Because he's paying you."

"Because it's fun."

He turned around then. "The chalice is in a vault in the very center of a wizard's complex, that requires getting through locks, motion sensors, and biosensors. And if you get any one part of that wrong, the security spells on the vault will liquify you before you have a chance to gasp. All of that is after we've made our way through the ever-changing spells in the rest of the building that will kill us if our ID cards stop working for some reason."

"Like I said. Fun."

"How are you still alive?"

She chuckled. "The fact that I am should tell you something."

He huffed out a groan and glanced away, before giving her a once over. "You're sleeping in your clothes?"

"You are, too." She nodded to his jeans. He even still had his shirt on. Which was a pity. But probably good for keeping her on her side of the suite.

"Just in case."

She nodded. "Same."

His gaze swept the length of her again, and his blue eyes darkened, a faint purple glow coloring the blue. "Shame."

Oh. Wow, did that start the tingles in her stomach again. And those tingles were moving lower. "Definitely a shame." But necessary. At least for tonight.

She slipped back to her side of the suite and pulled herself up onto the narrow top bunk without bothering with the ladder. She glanced back to see Christopher watching her from his side of the room, his expression impossible to read, his arms crossed over his chest. His sleeves were pushed up. He had very nice forearms.

She sat on the edge of the bed, her legs dangling down, her body folded forward to accommodate the low ceiling, bracing her hands on the edge of the bed, waiting for Christopher to speak. When he didn't say anything after a few moments, she raised her brows in question.

His expression went through a series of subtle shifts, none of which she could read, until he finally shook his head and turned back to his own bunk. Leaving her hanging. So to speak. Rude.

He hopped up onto the top bunk without much effort, and with no help from the little pull-down ladder either.

"Show off," she said.

"Just keeping up with you." The bed groaned under his weight.

She winced. "Hope that holds you. Maybe you should sleep on the lower bed."

"I'll be fine." He adjusted himself so he was laying on his side and could look down the narrow corridor at her.

That put his head toward the door, which made her twitchy. "You can sleep with your head pointing the other way if that makes you more comfortable." She gestured at the door.

"I prefer this. If someone comes through the door, I can reach their head better." He reached his hand out and made a sort of cupping gesture to mimic grabbing someone by the head just in front of the door.

She blinked. Huh. Having a dragon shifter guarding the door was a new experience. Little scary. Little thrilling.

"Whatever makes you comfortable, then." She rolled onto her own bunk, her back against the wall, her body curled up tight and angled so she could see the door but her head wasn't near it. She didn't have Christopher's grip.

Her position meant she couldn't see him anymore, with the bathrooms in the way, but if she listened quietly, she could still hear him breathing.

A few moments passed in silence. Then, "You can sleep, Myra. I'll make sure no one gets in."

She grinned up at the dark ceiling. "You need sleep, too."

"Not as much as you."

"Never had a dragon shifter bodyguard before."

His response was very quiet, so she wasn't sure if she was supposed to hear it. "Get used to it."

Her smile softened. A dragon prince bodyguard would probably cause a whole lot of trouble. But it didn't sound too awful. So long as the dragon prince in question was Christopher.

Six

yra snoozed a little, waiting until it was the early hours of the night—or morning depending on your perspective—before she slipped from the bunk, slid into her shoes, and snuck out of the sleeper car. She was pretty sure the person she was looking for was in coach, but she had a few cars to check.

She'd only gotten a glimpse of him during dinner. Long enough to know she and Christopher were being followed. Whoever he was, he was pretty good. Stayed to finish his meal after she and Christopher stood to leave. Didn't show her and Christopher a lot of attention.

Unfortunately for him, that had been the giveaway.

With so many other people in that dining car staring at Christopher, whispering about Christopher throughout the meal, the fact that that one lone diner never even once turned to see what all the fuss was about. Never glanced their way. Never looked at them on the way out of the dining car, even when they passed…

Well, that had been too obvious to go unnoticed.

Myra did wonder if Christopher had spotted the tail. Or maybe even sniffed him out. He didn't seem like the type to miss that sort of thing. But he was also the type who got himself kidnapped by enemies because he'd tried to save a woman he thought was in trouble and walked—or in his case, flown—into a trap. Given that he did have a blind spot like that, she couldn't be sure he'd realized the issue.

And she hadn't mentioned it because, in all honesty, she wanted to talk to this tail on her own, without the rather intimidating presence of the dragon king's son looming over her.

She moved through the coach cars on silent feet, passengers on either side of the aisle stretched out in their individual seats, tucked up under blankets, sleeping. The occasional insomniac or night owl or just someone who couldn't sleep sitting up, with their faces in their laptops or phones, the light casting weird multicolored shadows across their features in the otherwise dark train car. Outside the train, the countryside flashed past, the occasional clump of lights on the horizon to mark distant towns.

There wasn't a lot of warning before she came upon their tail. He was sitting in the aisle seat behind a couple of sleeping women, his eyes closed and head leaning back against the chair headrest, his legs stretched out under the seat in front of him, his own chair knocked back a little, but not in full recline. The seat next to him by the window was empty. The seat across the aisle from him occupied by a man who was snoring.

She spotted the tail in one breath, had just enough time to realize who he was, and in the next breath, he opened his eyes, looking right at her.

She grinned, waved her fingers at him, and easily slipped over the top of him to settle into the seat next to him, lightly using the seat backs of the sleeping women in front of him and his own to lever herself up and over. Her move must have surprised him because he didn't immediately do anything. Didn't reach for her or even try to run away. He blinked at her for a few startled moments. Which gave her another few seconds to study him.

Not a large man. About half the size of

Christopher in both height and width. A white man with light hair, cut neat and short, dark eyes, and a very narrow face. He was innocuous enough, the sort of person who could blend into a crowd. Go unnoticed. Not handsome. Not ugly. Nothing startling about his appearance at all. No tattoos that were visible around his ordinary clothes—jeans and a long sleeved, dark colored sweater—and no obvious jewelry except a gold band on his right pointer finger. Not a wedding ring, unless he just wore it on the wrong finger, and not an expensive piece of jewelry. Simple gold, not gold plated, but if she were a judge of these things—and she was—she'd say not high-quality gold either.

Outside of the ring, there were no distinguishing features to make him stand out. Nothing a person might glance at and latch onto as something they'd remember having seen before.

His bad luck that she had a great memory for faces and noticed small details as part of her career.

"Did the dragon king send you to follow us or someone else?" she whispered, turning in the seat so her legs were tucked up to her chest and she was half sitting on the armrest by the window, facing him directly while he turned awkwardly in his seat to face her.

The fact that he didn't run away was interesting. And he didn't immediately attack her when she questioned him. Also interesting.

"Not the king you're thinking about," he said.

"You're not a dragon, though." At least, she didn't think he was or Christopher would have spotted him earlier.

"I'm not."

"Why's the Chicago king having us tailed?"

"He's heard rumors."

"I *love* a good rumor. Do tell." She waggled her eyebrows at the man and leaned in.

A human, but not a wizard, she thought. No tingling sense of someone else's magic. And he hadn't thrown up a shield or tried to toss any magic at her. Most wizards she'd encountered—the few she'd had the bad luck to come up against—were quick with the spell casting.

And most wizards had a sort of burnt ozone smell to them, at least in her experience. She was able to wield her particular brand of magic without that scent following her around, but it was mostly because her magic and her spells didn't tend to burn up ozone when cast. Wizards liked to throw around things that sizzled. She just finessed locks and hid her own scent.

The man next to her just smelled like…well, nothing to her. Just ordinary, like the train. Maybe a little sweat? But otherwise, nothing in particular.

So she was going to say ordinary human. Which made sense if the Chicago king wanted to hire someone who could walk around and follow a dragon unnoticed.

"Rumors that one of the New York king's sons might be coming this way," the man said. "Maybe looking to interfere in some…negotiations the king is having with his people."

"Oh, I doubt that last one holds any water," she said. "Why would he want to do that?" She leaned in closer and lowered her voice, as if they were two old friends exchanging gossip.

The man's eyes narrowed, but he said, "Why else would someone like a prince be heading to Chicago now?"

"Vacation? Weekend getaway?"

"Not into another dragon king's territory. Not when you're the son of another king. And not in the company of a notorious thief."

"Notorious? Me?" She'd have assumed this guy didn't know who she was, though she did have a reputation. But since he did seem to know who she was… "What have you heard?"

"Managed to break into the New York king's hoard."

That was going to follow her around. She was inordinately proud that she'd managed it, but inordinately embarrassed that she'd been caught in the act. So it was hard to preen at having done something most thought impossible.

"Think that's me, huh?"

"We know it was you," the man said. "Impressive."

Would have been more impressive if she'd gotten out unnoticed.

"And you survived," the man added. "Was the bet worth it?"

"I survived," she said with a shrug. But she was annoyed he knew as much as he did. More dangerous, then. And that meant she'd been right to come out and confront him. "What are you intending? Why follow us?"

"I'm not supposed to kill you, if that's what you're worried about."

"Good to know."

"My job is just to see what you do."

"And if we don't want someone seeing what we do?"

He shrugged. "You might be better off just letting the Chicago king know your plans. He'll be less inclined to interfere. Especially if he knows it has nothing to do with his current… politics."

"Politics." Good euphemism for near rebellion in the Chicago king's cohort. "We've got no political interests."

"The Chicago king will want you to make a formal appearance," the man said.

"Of course he would. But we're just here on a weekender. Won't be around long enough for a visit with the king."

"Lovers' getaway?" the man asked.

She kept her expression controlled, but for some reason, that guess hit a little too close to home and made her jittery. "Sure." She tried for a casual shrug.

Must have succeeded in keeping her reaction to herself because the man's eyes narrowed slightly, like he couldn't quite make out whether she was admitting to an affair with Christopher or not.

"You gonna keep trying to follow us?"

"Just doing my job."

"You going to step in and interfere in any of our touristing?"

"Not my job."

"Then we have an understanding." She hopped back over the top of him into the aisle, moving fast enough to make him blink up at her. "Should have gotten the dragon king to at least spring for a roomette for you."

"I prefer coach," the man said, trying to recover from her sudden change of position without looking like he was trying to recover from her sudden change of position. "Easier to keep on eye on things."

"Kind of is, isn't it?" She touched a finger to her forehead in a little solute. "Sleep well."

She slipped silently back down the aisle past the sleeping passengers.

She didn't yelp when a hand grabbed her arm in the gangway between cars, but only because she'd been expecting him.

"What did he say?" Christopher asked near her ear, having hauled her close so they weren't in view through the car window.

"Chicago king sent him. He's just a tail, though. No orders to interfere."

She glanced up at Christopher. It was quite dark in the gangway, so all she could see about his expression were his glittering blue eyes. Even with her excellent night vision. Just two glowing blue eyes with a hint of purple, irises that looked to have more facets and angles than typical human eyes, the pupil narrowed now like a cat's. In the darkness, his glowing eyes were both compelling and terrifying. Especially since she couldn't really see the rest of his expression.

"Should we shake him?"

They could. Get off the train early. Now even. But she had a slightly different plan. "Not yet. Soon, though."

But things on this already interesting job had just gotten more interesting.

Seven

They made an appearance at breakfast, where Myra made sure their tail saw them even though he was still trying to be discrete. The dragon king of Chicago hired good people.

The dining car was quiet as she and Christopher had chosen to eat early. Their tail was already there, which made her wonder how long exactly he'd been sitting in the dining car, nursing a coffee. The meal was a decent collection of eggs and cooked meats and toast. Christopher, somewhat to her surprise, didn't like eggs. To no one's surprise, the dragon did eat a lot of the meat put in front of him.

There were less whispers this morning. Too many people too tired and up too early to bother with gossip, but Christopher still drew the gazes of those around them.

She forced herself to sit still through a second cup of coffee and to watch some of the passing scenery, attempting to appear calm and unconcerned that they were being watched and followed. Both she and the tail knew what was happening. He'd know Christopher was aware of his presence now, too. But all three of them were doing a bang-up job of appearing to ignore each other. It was pretty impressive, really, if Myra did say so herself.

By the time she and Christopher left the dining car, though, she was ready to move. She was capable of sitting still. She did often. Or maybe sometimes. But when she was excited, she didn't sit still very well. She gave their tail a little wave on the way out, which startled him into waving back. She grinned at his scowl.

Once back in their suite, without even speaking, she and Christopher gathered up their small backpacks—the extent of their luggage— and bid goodbye to the small cabin. Christopher removed his shirt as they walked down the narrow corridor, stuffed it into his backpack, then slung the pack over his shoulders, centering it. Unlike her wider pack, his was long, and narrow, and not like a normal human backpack. His sat along his spine, leaving lots of room around his shoulder blades.

She studiously ignored the fact that he was shirtless, more amused by the fact that he'd shucked off his shoes the instant they'd returned from their meal and those were already inside his pack. He really didn't like wearing shoes.

At the gangway at the rear of the train, where there were currently no train staff, Myra hunted up the emergency hatch. The thing most people didn't know even existed, but which allowed access to the roof of the train. If she'd been on her own, she'd have had to use some sticky grips on the walls and ceiling to climb up to the hatch and get it open. But with Christopher here…

"Boost me up," she said, turning her back to him. He lifted her by the waist, holding her up as if she weighed less than his shoes. There went those stomach tingles again.

She finessed the alarm set on the hatch with a small spell and then pulled the handle out and down, pushing up on the heavy chunk of metal. That was harder than it sounded because the train was still in motion and that hatch was working against the air friction of highspeed rail travel. She scrambled through the hatch the instant it was open, staying low to the roof of the train and using a couple of her sticky grips to give her secure handholds so she wasn't swept off the fast-moving vehicle.

Once Christopher had pulled himself up and closed the hatch—with impressive ease—she released the spell that held the grips firmly to the slick metal roof and tucked them back into one of the many pockets in her fitted black vest.

The countryside around them flew past, mostly farmlands now. And from here, they had a good view of the lake. The train would arrive in Chicago in only a couple of more hours. Soon they'd be traveling through outer suburbs and the small towns that circled Chicago. In maybe another twenty minutes, they'd pass through one of those towns.

She wanted to be off the train before they got there. And their exit point was approaching fast.

When she faced Christopher again, he was scowling at her, also low to the roof in deference to the wind speed pulling at them.

"You sure about this?" he asked, shouting to be heard above the noise of the train and icy cold wind.

She grinned. "It'll be fun."

She tugged down the straps of her backpack, ensuring it was secured. Then she stood, the wind buffeting her and rocking her on her feet. She looked over the side of the train. Smiled at Christopher. And leapt up and to the right.

A move that took her out over a steep drop into a valley as the train passed over a bridge.

The sharp change in position and motion rocked her and sent her tumbling, making the freefall hard to enjoy. But she didn't have long to enjoy it anyway. An instant, just long enough to take a deep breath, and then strong arms caught around her back and under her legs, scooping her up.

She grinned up at Christopher's face as he focused on the landscape ahead. His huge wings spread out above them, a shimmering purple that reflected the sun. The light filtered through the thin membranes between thick, trailing bones and the small, more delicate looking bones that stretched like fingers down through the width of his wings. There were little hooks, like fingers at the first joint of the main trailing bone, which were black among the thick iridescent purple and yellow scales.

More purple and yellow scales spread across his chest now, along his collarbone and over his shoulders in a delicate pattern. The partial shift didn't affect much more of him, except for the soles of his feet becoming thicker. Given the beauty of his wings, she was really curious what he'd looked like as full dragon.

He banked out over the valley, catching an air current and pumping his wings in several strong beats to get them higher, above the bridge and train, skimming across the tree tops before rising higher. When they'd reached an altitude he deemed comfortable enough for her to breathe but still put them above the trees and farms, she glanced down at the ground far below, awed by the view. Even from airplanes, she wouldn't get this view, this ability to look straight down to the ground without anything but a dragon shifter's wings keeping her up here.

She straightened and tightened her arms around his neck, ensuring she was secure enough for him to adjust his arm around her back, so it was beneath the backpack instead of across it. The new position put his hand down by her waist. She liked his hand on her waist.

She was also now level with the side of his head, close enough to see he'd shaved very well that morning.

She grinned. "See," she said. "Fun."

He let out a long breath as he banked toward the distant city. She couldn't tell if he was trying to contain a smile or a scowl.

EIGHT

Ditching their tail on the train and flying the last few hours to the city proved one of the more unique experiences of Myra's life. One that, in all honestly, she wasn't sure she'd repeat.

Because, as it turned out, she loved flying with Christopher. She felt surprisingly secure and safe, trusted him a lot more than she probably should to not drop her. And that was a problem. Too easy to get used to the cold air whipping through her hair, across her cheeks, the sound of his strong wings occasionally pumping above them, the flutter of air rippling across the thin membranes like a breeze across canvas sails, his body heat keeping her comfortable despite the cold wind of their passage. Even the smell of fresh air and Christopher…

The experience was all so delightful and fun. And fast.

And getting used to it, perhaps even starting to rely on it, would be very very bad.

He landed in a park on the outskirts of the city, but within walking distance to an "L" station, remaining cloaked until they were on the ground and he'd tucked his wings away. Now that they were here, she did worry that flying in might have alerted the dragon shifters that Christopher was in town. The cloaking kept humans from noticing them. She had no idea if dragon cloaks worked on other dragons.

But since the Chicago king had already been tracking him, the dragons here already knew he was on his way. The tail had probably called the Chicago king already to let him know Christopher was off the train and likely flying in.

The dragons were just something they'd have to deal with. But hopefully not until after they'd finished swiping the chalice from the wizard.

Things went smoothly getting her DNA-matched ID card for the building. This wasn't her first time pretending to be cleaning staff. She knew how to play that role believably.

After a great deal of debate—and her search

coming up empty on a dragon shifter that bore a close enough physical resemblance to Christopher to pass—she talked Christopher into remaining outside of the building while she went in. It was not an easy conversation. Everything in him rebelled at letting her go in alone and she knew it. But without an ID card, he'd die.

And now that they knew the Chicago king was aware of their presence in town, she worried the dragons inside the building would recognize Christopher instantly, even if they'd managed to score him an ID.

He couldn't wait for her on the roof of the building itself, because it was bespelled with dangerous security magic, too. But she compromised and agreed he could wait for her on a neighboring roof, keeping watch in case her escape plan went sideways.

They wasted some scouting time having this argument, but by eight that night, she was heading into the huge skyscraper in downtown Chicago, a few blocks from the lake, the "L" loop rumbling past just outside the windows on the third floor.

As an employee and cleaner, she entered through a side door, not the main lobby, but like the rest of the building it was protected by spells. If she entered without her ID card, she'd be dissolved. She hesitated before stepping onto the black linoleum floors in the employee lobby, a momentary thrill of fear coursing through her blood.

The security guard at the door, a human woman, said, "You got your card, it's okay, honey. Don't worry. It takes some getting used to for all new hires, but once you do, it's just like working anywhere else. Cleaning's cleaning, right?"

Myra nodded, let out a breath, and stepped into the smaller employee lobby. Smiled at the security guard when nothing happened

"Told you," the guard said with a wink. "Good luck."

Myra thanked her and hurried to the employee elevator and the maintenance office where the cleaners were assigned floors and the cleaning equipment was kept.

So far so good.

Now she just had to get the chalice.

The good thing about working as a cleaner was that most people didn't look up long enough to register a face. Even the friendly people rarely took the time to talk long with someone popping in to clean their office. At this time of night, the day shifts were gone and there were only a few people working late. It was, to her outsider's view, just like any other downtown office building, mostly busy during ordinary work hours and only the ambitious or reluctant to go home staying late into the evening.

Given that a wizard owned this place, she suspected more people were willing to go home than stay, though, based on the relative emptiness of the offices. If she had to worry about her employee card fritzing and accidentally getting fried by magical spells, she'd go home on time every night, too.

Pushing her cart full of cleaning supplies, brooms, mops, and a garbage bag stretched open over one side through the building ensured no one gave her a second glance, though she did get the occasional wave or half smile before people turned their attention back to their phones or inner thoughts.

She walked past a patrol of dragon guards, as well, but none of them paid any attention to her. They made themselves obvious by wearing uniform dress shirts with an embroidered golden dragon on the back. Not very subtle. She ensured she memorized their faces. Knowing the ones working here were dragons that didn't like the Chicago king gave her a bit of information to file away for later use. Always good for a thief to have important information in her mental files.

The elevator down to the subterranean floor where the vault was located was empty, but she continued to play the role of a half disinterested cleaner because cameras were a thing. Someone was watching her. And the more disinterested she was, the more disinterested the watcher would be in what she was doing.

She was a passible computer hacker—part of a thief's job in the modern era—but she hadn't been able to get at the vault cameras from outside the building. So she was going to have to finesse them on the ground. She couldn't bring in a disposable laptop to help with that either, because of the metal detectors getting into the building—what would a cleaner need with a laptop?—and navigating the kill spells everywhere was challenging enough. She'd have to rely on her magic. Her spell for finessing the cameras wasn't as reliable as a physical hack, but it worked in a pinch.

She rolled her cart off the elevator and made her way directly to one of the offices near the vault. There were no connections to the vault from that office that weren't covered in spells, but she had to get rid of the cart and fix the security cameras, and there was a camera in the office she could use to spell into those monitoring the vault.

The space was a windowless square with slick black conference desk in the center that didn't even have any chairs around it. There were some boxes stacked against one wall, that she investigated as she was pretending to dust, but they were mostly blank printer paper. There were high vents in the room, for the connecting air ducts, but those would be spelled, and the carpets were well worn and smelled vaguely like spilled coffee.

It was a depressingly dark sort of room with one overhead florescent light and walls painted an unfortunate steel gray. She had no idea what the room might normally be used for, but she was guessing hatching evil plans to take over the world because why else would anyone have a room this ugly and depressing tucked away in a basement level of the building.

Or maybe it was just supposed to be a storage room that had never fully materialized. Hard to say. And she didn't really care. Once she'd dusted around to the cameras, she slipped the powder from her pants pocket and sprinkled it onto the fluffy fake feather duster. She missed having on her vest with all the pockets, but the cleaner's uniform of tan pants and a short-sleeved navy shirt were a required disguise.

As she dusted the camera with her spell, she wondered how Christopher was doing. What he was doing. Was he sticking to his promise to remain on the building across the road? Had he spotted anything from that lookout perch that might be important? Not having a handy way to communicate was a pain. But she wasn't used to working with anyone else, so she'd forgotten to pick up some of those handy earpieces that would allow them to talk. Probably for the best anyway. She wasn't sure if those would have made it through the security metal detectors unnoticed. And having Christopher constantly asking if she was okay in her ear would be distracting.

Not that she could be certain that's what he'd do. But he was totally the type to clutter up the communications line with checking to make sure everything was going to plan. And there was only so often she'd be able to say yes without getting annoyed. Especially since she certainly wasn't going to answer that question with a no and risk the disaster of him swooping in to try and rescue her. That had worked that one time but was more likely to get them both killed in this situation.

Once she was certain the camera spell had had sufficient time to set, she pushed her cart to a spot under the camera, where it wasn't visible, and waited for the spell to get a loop of the supposedly empty room that it would play on repeat after she left. She had to wait out the spell doing the same for the hall cameras and the cameras outside the vault.

The spell wasn't full proof, because someone could walk through the shot at just exactly the wrong time, creating a loop of that person moving through the frame in the exact same way over and over again. But this level was supposedly empty, so she was betting the odds.

As she waited, she stripped off the cleaner's uniform, reached under the stack of folded garbage bags on her cart, and redressed in her happy clothes. The black leggings and her multi-pocket vest that were *her* uniform.

After ten minutes, she slipped from the office and went directly to the vault. If her spell hadn't worked, she'd know soon enough when either she liquified from a triggered magic spell or a collection of dragon guards came to collect her. Neither prospect sounded fun. But risks had to be taken in these kinds of jobs. Especially when under a time crunch.

The vault was behind a pretty typical looking door. Round like a bank vault's door, shiny silver steel gleaming under another single florescent light. A multi-layered lock panel that required both biometric scans and a passcode next to a large, multi-pronged wheel for spinning and opening the huge round door. The model was one she'd worked on before, though, so that was one extra layer of research she'd been able to shortcut.

She stood outside the vault, anticipation crawling through her gut, waiting for some signal that she'd been caught. Her ears strained to hear any sound of approaching feet. She'd disguised her scent the moment she was no longer having to pass as a cleaner—if the dragons hadn't picked up a scent from her that would have immediately given her away—but it wasn't her scent that would bring down trouble now.

When she managed to survive those few minutes, and no one came running in to snatch her up, she grinned and went to work on the vault lock. There were spells here, too, but surprisingly, the wizard had relied on the surrounding spells to protect the vault and only inserted a few electrical charge spells onto the door lock. Probably that was a good use of energy. Given the nature of the surrounding spells, and the inability to even get this far in the building without dying if you weren't welcome, wasting power on complicated locking spells probably seemed like overkill.

The spells were easier to finesse than the lock itself. Which took her fifteen seconds longer to crack than she'd accounted for. Fifteen seconds she was going to have to make up somewhere. The heavy locks clicked, the giant tubes of steel pulled out of the interlocking panels in the surrounding walls with a chunking sound, and the door popped open an inch, release a hiss of air.

She never celebrated until she'd gotten the thing she came to steal and escaped, but she did allow a satisfied smile as she wedged the huge door open enough for her to slip inside.

The interior of the vault was a steel-lined square with tiny air vents up at the roof that were so small, nothing larger than a mouse could slip through them and were on their own system, cut off from the rest of the building, the air in here constantly circulating through its independent filtering cycle. A good filter system because the air inside the vault was fresh and crisp. Even a little cold. Actually, very cold, she realized. They had the temperature inside so low she could see her breath.

She hadn't planned on that. Temperature affected a lot of things, including spotting heat signatures on surveillance systems. But there wasn't a heat sensor on this room that she could find in the specs. Maybe the temperature was important to something they had stored here?

She looked around. There wasn't a lot visible inside the vault. There were a series of small cubbies along one wall, like in a security deposit box section of a bank. A miniature version of the main vault door directly across from the entrance, with a series of blinking electronic locks and another biosensor panel. And a plain steel wall opposite the bank of security box cubbies. Nothing in the center of the black marble floor. Not even a logo or other distinguishing feature. There were motion detectors in the floor, but those were only activated when the vault was locked, even though slipping into this model of vault without going through the door was impossible— she'd tried multiple ways. Never worked. This vault, you needed to get in through the big, round, steel door.

She started toward the mini-vault door at the opposite side of the chamber, but her curiosity about what was stored in those cubbies along the wall to her left almost had her exploring. There wasn't enough time to spend on that. The whole operation was timed to the second to ensure she didn't cross over any of the dragon guard patrols, and she'd already lost a few of those seconds on the vault lock. Which was unfortunate. She would have liked to have seen what those boxes held since she hadn't been able to find that in her research. Probably just jewels and money and bonds. Although, it could be spells, since this was a wizard's tower. Or bespelled objects. Maybe that's why it was so damned cold in here.

She forced herself away from the wall of cubbies and to the mini vault door.

This one took her another extra thirty seconds to finesse, which irritated the hell out of her. It wasn't the lock this time, though. Getting the biosensors to register her spelled signature took that tiny bit longer than it should have.

There was that moment, that gut-churning, heart-pounding, adrenaline-spiking moment when she worried the spells would fail and the alarms would sound. Honestly, she sort of loved those moments. The rush was incredible.

The rush was even stronger and more satisfying when the locks finally clicked open, and the miniature vault door hissed open.

She grinned, swinging it wide…

To be confronted with betrayal.

NINE

She met Christopher on the roof of a building downtown, opposite side of the "L" loop from the wizard's tower. The high-rise gave a great view of the lake in one direction, the brightly lit night landscape of downtown Chicago in the opposite direction. The "L" rumbled past far below, screeching against the tracks as it made the turn. There were shorter buildings bumping up against this one, but this one stood tall enough, and had a flat enough roof, to make it easy for a dragon to land.

He was already waiting for her when she arrived, so she wasn't sure if he came in on wings or just used the elevator the way she had. But honestly, she was too pissed off to care.

"He lied," she said, stomping up to Christopher where he sat on the low, stone wall circling the roof, his back to the lake. "Your father lied."

"He does that a lot. I thought you knew he had."

"I knew he lied about aspects of this job," she said, slowly, through her teeth. "What I didn't realize he'd lied about is that there is no chalice here. He sent me on a wild goose chase."

"What?" Christopher straightened. "What are you talking about? The wizard moved the chalice?"

"No. There never was a chalice. It isn't now, nor has it ever been, in the wizard's possession."

"How could you know that? Your own research showed the chalice was there, that the wizard had it."

"And that's a mistake I intend to check into," she said, her cheeks hot that he'd pointed out her own mistake. "How I know he never had it... After I searched every cubby in the vault and nearly got caught slipping out—"

"Are you okay?" He stepped closer to her, but she waved him away.

"That's not the point. I got out. The other lock boxes were mostly empty. There were a few with spells. And one with a relic that I may go back for one day. But no bone and dragon skin chalice. Nothing even resembling a cup."

"What was in the lock box where the chalice was supposed to be?"

"A book. A thick, leatherbound book. A book of spells. The *exact* sort of thing a wizard would store in his most guarded safe. Not a dragon relic. A *wizard* relic. What I'd expect to find in a wizard's safe." She shook her head and cursed, stalking away from Christopher, then stalking back. "No chalice anywhere," she repeated. "So on my way out, I snuck into one of the offices with a computer that had security access. There was never a chalice here. Ever. It's never been on the inventory, isn't part of the security precautions. It. Was. Never. There. I'm not sure the wizard even knows what it is or that it exists. If he does, he's not looking for it."

Christopher's brows lowered, giving him an expression most people would call deadly and probably terrifying. She was too angry to be scared. And a part of her knew she never had to be scared of Christopher, that he'd never physically hurt her. It was a weird bit of knowledge, given she'd known him for less than a week, and she was so fucking angry she could barely think straight.

"I don't understand."

"Me neither. Why the hell did your father send us into the territory of one of his rivals, where you're in danger—and he had to know, given your soft spot for women in a fix, that you'd go with me. He set us up to infiltrate a wizard's tower in the middle of a rival king's territory, when there's infighting going on between the dragons and…"

She trailed off and scowled at the stone roof as her mind worked, churning through what she'd learned and seen. What she knew now that she hadn't before. A cold breeze off the river blew through her hair, brushing strands that had escaped her tight braid across her forehead. She swiped them away.

When she looked up again, Christopher was scowling at her. "Your father is a devious, sneaky bastard."

"He has to be to lead a dragon cohort. He wouldn't have stayed king long if he wasn't devious and sneaky. But I swear, I didn't know he'd lied about the chalice. I thought this was an honest job. The chalice has been missing for decades. I thought he'd finally found it."

"He might have found the chalice somewhere, but it wasn't here. That's not why he sent us."

"Why do you think he send us, then?"

Before she could answer, a dark shadow

swooped across them from overhead, cutting off the nightlight for a few moments, an icy gust of wind battering the rooftop as the sound of snapping wings drew both Myra and Christopher's gazes up.

The dragon circled overhead, a full-grown adult dragon with a wing span that blocked out the sky, a thick body, long tail, and suspiciously sharp looking spikes around its long, slim neck. Against the city lights, the dragon was a dark color, maybe blue but possibly red. And its scales caught the building lights, giving it a shimmering glow.

Something that large should not be able to fly in between the tightly packed skyscrapers of downtown Chicago, but dragons, Myra was learning, were amazing creatures with an awful lot more maneuverability than she'd assumed given their size.

The dragon tucked its wings and slid between the high buildings to the north of them, before circling back and landing on the opposite side of the roof, facing them. Up close, the creature was even more intimidatingly impressive, with a long face circled by a sharp-looking ruff of what could be spikes or hair, raised nostrils that steamed, and wide set, black eyes that were impossible to read.

Somewhat to Myra's amusement, Christopher

moved to stand in front of her, placing himself between the strange dragon and her. He really was very gallant. It was weird to be on the receiving end of all that gallantry, though.

Because he was guarding their front from the dragon, she took a moment to glance over the side of the building. Long way down to the sidewalk.

She faced the dragon again as it shifted and shrank, its body shimmering in a cloud of sparkling dark fog as it made the change. That was…wild. To be fair, she'd never seen a dragon shift from full dragon to human before. The closest she'd gotten was watching Christopher snap out wings when he needed them.

Again, it occurred to her she hadn't seen Christopher's full dragon form yet. And she was curious enough to wonder what he'd look like.

When the stranger dragon finished its shift, Myra wasn't really surprised to see their tail from the train. She *was* a little surprised he really was a dragon. She'd been prepared to believe he was human as he'd claimed because Christopher hadn't sniffed him out as a dragon. She'd have to ask Christopher about that later. She was also a little surprised the newcomer had approached them in full dragon regalia after trying to pass as human on the train. He could have just used the elevator like she had.

His human form was the same as it had been on the train, so he really did look that way as a human. Innocuous, light hair, dark eyes. Smaller than Christopher in stature, but taller standing than she'd thought on the train. He had clothes on after the shift, which she found interesting. Christopher took his shirt off to let his wings out. Was that only because it was a partial shift or…?

So many questions about dragon shifters. Really, she needed to do more research.

"Long time no see," she called to the man. "You said you weren't a dragon."

"And you said you were here for a vacation," he said, walking slowly toward them, his hands open and at his sides.

She assumed he was trying to look harmless, or at least like he wasn't intending on attacking them. But honestly, he'd landed on the roof in dragon form. Did he really think he'd get away with looking harmless now?

"But you already knew that was a lie," she said. "Are you working with the New York king after all?"

His gaze flicked to Christopher, who'd remained silent and firmly between her and the new dragon. "Not…technically. I was being honest about that at least."

"Oh, I'd love to hear this. Go on. You're here

for a reason. Spill the tea and tell us all the gossip."

"We needed a distraction," the dragon said with a shrug. "And information."

"Meaning?" Christopher asked. Given that was the first word he'd spoken, and his voice was very deep and guttural sounding, with just a hint of hiss in it even though there were no "s"s in the word, Myra thought maybe the new dragon should be nervous.

The dragon did flick a quick look at Christopher, then focused his gaze on Myra, his head tilted down at an angle that made it necessary for him to look upward to meet her eyes. It was a strange and awkward sort of angle. She had to assume he was doing that on purpose. And suddenly it occurred to her that might be some sort of dragon deference gesture?

"The wizard is siding with the rebelling dragons in this situation. He's been here in Chicago a long time, and he's always worked here at the dragon king's pleasure. We suspect he'd like to change that balance."

"That's a you guys thing," Myra said. "Why would the *New Yor*] king send us here? Send *me* here?" Especially for so much money, to retrieve something that wasn't here, to help another king. None of it made sense.

"It's to the New York king's benefit to monitor what's happening in Chicago and, if possible, to ensure dragons don't get the idea that rebelling against their king is a viable option."

She could see that. "What's your name?" she asked suddenly. Tired of looking at this guy and thinking of him as a tail. That took on a new meaning when he was a dragon shifter and actually had a tail.

"Archer."

"If I call you Archie, will you growl?"

"Yes."

"Fair enough. He has to be Christopher." She nodded at Christopher, who growled if you tried to call him Chris. Which was fine. She liked Christopher better. "Is that a dragon thing? Not liking your names shortened?"

"You don't know?"

"Why would I?"

Archer paused, then shrugged. "Right." Again his gaze flicked to Christopher but very briefly before dancing away.

"So, why bring in a human thief and risk sending Christopher here? Still not seeing the connection." Actually, she was starting to. But she wanted the explanation from the dragon's mouth, so to speak, to make sure she'd figured this out right.

"Christopher made for a good distraction. The dragons here are whispering. The rebelling ones worried the New York king might involve himself and his cohort."

"Would he?" she asked Christopher. "Seems the kings usually stay out of this sort of thing." Not that she really knew. Archer had made it abundantly clear she wasn't overflowing with the dragon knowledge.

"I hadn't thought he would," Christopher said. "But given this… I'll have to speak with him when we return."

Oh, she'd love to be a fly on the wall during that conversation. Though, if things got spicy and they started throwing fire at each other, she wouldn't want to be caught in that crossfire.

"Christopher is only here because the New York king sent me to retrieve a chalice that wasn't there. Why *that* part of all this?" Although, she'd already guessed.

"To test the wizard's defenses."

"Of course. And the fact that I got in and out?"

"Means he's not invulnerable."

"But also that I'm very very good at what I do and not just anyone and their dragon could have done what I did."

Archer shrugged. "Fair point. But if it's possible for anyone, then it's possible. Which means the wizard and all his dragons are not impervious to consequences while they're inside the wizard's tower."

"You used us."

"It's what kings do."

And she was not at all happy about it. Only good thing was she got paid up front. That money had already been moved to several separate and secret accounts so the king couldn't just snatch it back. Seems her natural paranoia worked in her favor on this job. Except for the part where she actually did a job that wasn't one.

"Now what?"

"You two can go home. Or stay for the weekend. The Chicago king has offered you the use of his suite at one of the luxury hotels if you'd like to use it." His gaze flicked to Christopher again. "Special guests."

"No," Christopher said before she could.

She might love the idea of staying in a luxury hotel for the night, and she definitely wouldn't mind exploring Chicago more at some point. This was not that moment.

She also flicked a glance at Christopher. She was still deciding if he was that company.

Archer just shrugged at Christopher's rejection of the Chicago king's offer. "Suit yourselves."

"Why can't he smell you?" she asked, curious.

"Why didn't Christopher know you were a dragon?"

"Ah. That. Well…"

"A genetic anomaly," Christopher answered for him. "Happens in about one in every thousand dragons. His dragon side doesn't create a scent. Just his human side. So dragons…all shifters really, will only register him as human."

"Is that…a good anomaly or a bad one?" she asked both dragons.

"Handy," Archer said. "Easier to fly under the radar. So to speak."

"They often work as intermediaries between cohorts because they don't trigger aggressive territorial instincts in different kings," Christopher added.

Ah. So that's how this all got set up. "You've been passing the messages between kings," she said. "And that's why you in particular where the one following us."

"Christopher wouldn't be able to identify me as a dragon, and I'm the only one outside of the kings who knew what your real mission was, so it made sense I keep an eye on you."

She pulled in a deep breath and let it out in a rush, letting it ruffle the fine hairs on her forehead. "I'd call this a wasted trip, but I got paid, and paid well, so I guess that's something."

"And you managed to break into a wizard's tower and escape unscathed," Archer pointed out.

She wanted to wave that away, but given the wizard's guard spells, she was pretty proud of that accomplishment.

"Since you're not staying the weekend, the Chicago king has something for the New York king. Save me a trip if you could bring it back to him."

Christopher growled low in his throat, which Myra decided meant she needed to do the talking here. "We'll deliver this whatever it is, but that's gonna cost extra. Courier fee."

Archer's mouth twitched. The closest he'd come to a smile. "You can bill the king. He's good for it."

"Which one?"

"Up to you. They've both got the funds."

"You trying to tempt me?"

"Didn't learn from the last bet you took to break into a dragon king's hoard?" Archer asked.

"Fair point. What are we delivering?"

Archer, his gaze fully on Christopher now, shrugged something off his shoulders, slowly.

Myra had noticed the straps over his shoulders, a backpack like the type Christopher wore, that was long and narrow down the spine, leaving room for wings. But she was pretty sure that backpack hadn't been on Archer's back in dragon form. At least, she hadn't noticed it while he was dragon. Though the big teeth and potential for fire breath might have distracted her.

Archer's movements remained slow, and careful, as he pulled the pack around and set it gently on the ground. He proceeded to open it very slowly, his gaze still directed toward Christopher. But now he was kneeling and his head was definitely tilted down. A very supplicant pose.

Myra watched it all, fascinated. She had so many questions. But mostly, just watching dragons interact with other dragons gave her a lot of information. She wondered if they realized they were revealing themselves to her. She also wondered if Christopher would answer some of her many questions.

The backpack fell open. Archer jumped away from the contents, suddenly enough to land about ten yards away.

Okay. She frowned and looked at what the open bag revealed.

Except…

She had to be seeing that wrong.

She leaned around Christopher to get a better look. Nope. She was absolutely seeing that right. Even if she hadn't trusted her own eyes, which she did—one of her magic skills made it easier for her to see through magical illusions—Christopher's quiet hiss would have confirmed her suspicions.

The chalice.

The very fucking chalice they'd been sent to steal.

TEN

"The Chicago king had it all along?" Myra asked without looking at Archer. Her full attention was on the huge cup sticking out of the crumbled black backpack sitting innocently on the roof of the high-rise, the lights of downtown Chicago surrounding them. A cold breeze off the lake ruffled her hair and she hardly noticed. She couldn't believe what she was seeing. And yet, she really should have guessed.

Fucking dragon kings.

"How do you think he paid for the New York king's help?" Archer said with a shrug she caught from the corner of her eye.

In real life, the chalice was a pretty impressive relic, even rising up out of the pile of nylon. It was larger than she'd realized, based on the pictures, probably a good two-foot-tall, with a flat, round base, long, thick stem—she'd have trouble getting one hand around it—and a wide, shallow bowl at the top. The rim around the bowl and the rounded base of polished white were the only visible bone parts of the chalice. The rest was wrapped in an iridescent, shimmering material that resembled green, yellow, and purple scales but also looked like stained glass. The skin of a dragon from centuries past, according to the legend around the chalice.

The scales were almost as see through as glass, giving hints of the bone structure underneath. In the pictures, that transparency had been difficult to see. The luminosity of it hard to appreciate. In person, the cup fairly glowed, even in the dim lights thrown by the surrounding skyscrapers. It almost looked like the cup was lit from within, like the skin had a natural luminescence.

It was one of the most beautiful cups she'd ever seen. And now that she was seeing it in person, she realized she'd have had trouble carrying that thing out of the wizard's tower. And also, it was entirely too big for the cubby safe it was supposed to have been in.

Honestly, she should have known she was being played sooner. It was just embarrassing that she hadn't figured it out before breaking into the vault.

"Pretty," she murmured, straightening.

"Dangerous," Christopher said.

"You get to carry it, then." She didn't trust the New York king at his word that touching the chalice wouldn't be bad for her. The scales were glowing. On a cup. Without any internal battery or light. The only things she knew that did that were magic and radiation, and neither seemed like a good idea to touch.

Christopher didn't immediately approach the bag. He stared hard at Archer, the intensity of the stare intimidating to Myra and she wasn't even the focus of it. She looked up at the side of his face. Yeah, he could probably be pretty scary when he wanted to be.

She didn't consider interfering, though. This was a dragon thing. And she couldn't breathe fire.

After several very tense moments, Christopher lowered his gaze to the backpack. "The king thanks you for your assistance in this matter," he said, very formally. "I take possession of the payment for *his* assistance in your matter. We are in accord."

"We are in accord," Archer repeated, his head bowed.

Christopher stalked forward suddenly and

Myra rushed to keep up. She wasn't going to touch the chalice, but she definitely wanted a closer look.

"That would have been tricky to carry out of the wizard's tower," she murmured, staring down at the huge goblet, that looked even larger up close. Definitely two-foot-tall, plus, and probably weighed fifty pounds or more. Unless there was some dragon magic that made it lighter than it looked.

Based on the flexing of Christopher's arm muscles as he lifted the entire backpack containing the chalice, she was guessing the cup might weigh even more than she thought.

"Could you have managed?" Christopher asked quietly as he stared at the relic. In his hands, the whole thing looked less massive, still huge, but more like it fit. Definitely a cup designed for dragons the size of Christopher.

"I could have managed. But it would have been trickier. The pictures didn't do it justice."

Christopher pulled the sides of the backpack up and zipped it closed, the chalice safely cut off from the outside world again. He slipped the whole thing over his back. He still had his shirt on, not taking it off when he positioned the pack, so he wasn't going to fly them off the roof.

That was a shame. She liked jumping off roofs.

"When you see them," Christopher said to Archer, "tell the rebels that I stand by what I said. I won't be helping them."

Myra bit her lip to keep from showing any reaction to what Christopher had just said.

Archer didn't show that same restraint. His brows went up high, even though his head remained mostly tilted down. "You assume I'll see them? I'm loyal to my king."

"I'm sure you are. Just pass on my message. I don't want to have to make my point again. Next time, I won't be so restrained."

Myra could actually see Archer swallowing. There were things going on in this conversation that she needed to understand better. But maybe after Archer left.

The other dragon gave a sharp nod, then backed up a few paces and started to shift. Christopher edged Myra backward, so there was distance between them and the changing shifter. Once Archer finished, the huge dragon stood across the roof from them, his wings tucked against his thick sides. Now that she could see him better this way, Myra noted the color of his scales was definitely red, but a dark maroon red.

The dragon, despite the size difference, dipped

his huge head at Christopher, then rose onto his hind legs, flapped his wings once, and launched straight upward. The wind from his wings forced Myra backward a step. Christopher caught her arm to keep her from falling over. She grinned up at him, shaking her head.

"You don't even think about that kind of thing, do you?"

"About what?" he asked, his gaze turned upward as he tracked the retreating dragon.

"Nothing." She waited until Archer had disappeared and Christopher looked down at her before asking, "So you met some of the rebel dragons while I was busy breaking into the wizard tower, huh?"

"They came and found me on the roof across from the wizard's tower while I was waiting for you, yes. Which is, I suspect, what both the kings were hoping for."

"What did they say?"

He shrugged and set a gentle hand at the small of her back, guiding her toward the door that would take them inside the building and to the elevator. "They are unhappy with the way their king is running things. They'd like a new king."

"Do they have someone in mind?"

"Me."

She stumbled over the doorway ledge leading

into the small foyer where the elevator and stairway were. Christopher caught her again with ease.

She was too surprised to be embarrassed by the slip. "You? You who is already the son of another territory's king?"

"A king who's strong and has good control of his cohort. By having me king here, they'd also get the power and backing of my father. So they assumed. For some reason, they thought that would be a good idea."

"I take it it's not."

They had to wait a few minutes for the elevator to come all the way up to them. The five-foot square foyer around them was utilitarian, gray walls, black linoleum flooring, all easy to clean but not designed to be aesthetically pleasing. She presumed because no one in the building used the roof for much. There was just enough room for her and Christopher to stand side-by-side, but it reminded her a little of the sleeper car on the train. Forcing them into close proximity, close enough to touch.

She didn't actually mind the touching part, though.

"Attempting to combine both cohorts under a dynastic kingship would be bad for everyone. My father has more than enough power as is. Anymore would be…dangerous."

Well. That was an interesting insight. The elevator bell dinged and the silver doors slid open. Christopher followed her inside, but he had to duck to get in.

"So," she said. "Back to New York. Your father gets the chalice after all. We leave the trouble in Chicago here in Chicago. And we go back to our regular lives?"

"What is your regular life?" he asked as the elevator whisked them down to the ground level.

She grinned. "More of this. But in New York mostly."

"And when you aren't stealing things?"

"I like to read." She folded her hands in front of her, smiling at their reflections in the elevator doors. "How about you?"

"Reading is nice. Movies are good, too."

"Go to many movies, do you?" She wondered if he could do movies without drawing so much attention they were impossible to enjoy. She also wondered if the seating would be uncomfortable for someone his size.

"The occasional matinee," he said.

"Sounds fun."

"Want to join me for a movie? After we get back."

Her grin widened. "So long as it's not a heist movie, I'm in."

"No crime movies? I'm surprised."

She shrugged. "I get enough crime in my day job."

Christopher's chuckle tickled along her spine and started that tingling in her stomach again. That tingling sensation was going to get her into trouble. Definitely dangerous.

Good thing she liked danger.

Thank You

Thank you for reading book two in the Dragon Thief series! I hope you enjoyed THE CHICAGO JOB. There's more to come with Myra and Christopher. Do they ever get that movie date? You'll have to pick up THE POISONS BOOK JOB to find out.

With a few series, it feels like all the things I've been reading, writing, learning, studying, all those things come together so that I can create something I wouldn't have been able to a few years earlier. This series is one of those. And I'm really enjoying writing in this world. It's also fun to break out of some of the world building I've done for other urban fantasy and paranormal romance series, and do a whole new thing here.

This is the only urban fantasy or paranormal romance I've published that can't cross over into any of the other worlds. This one is more alternate history. The dragons are here and public, and everyone knows they exist. That's a really interesting world to play in since in all my other worlds, the paranormal and otherworldly is hidden from average humans.

If you're interested in some of my other books, I'd recommend starting with the Cary Redmond series for urban fantasy—there's a healthy dose of romance in that one too, and more sexy shapeshifters. My Tiger Shifter series is paranormal romance, leans toward the hot end of the romance spectrum, and...well there are more sexy shapeshifters. I obviously love shapeshifter stories. Sexy shapeshifter stories. *grin*

For more on all my books, check out KatSimonsBooks or visit my website. You can also join my newsletter for up-to-date release information, excerpts, cover reveals, coupons to my store, and the occasional free read. New subscribers get two exclusive stories, not available anywhere else. One each in my Cary Redmond series and my Tiger Shifter series. If you prefer, you can follow my author page at BookBub, Facebook, or your favorite vendors. I can also occasionally be found on Instagram mostly talking about food and sporting events.

Thanks again for reading THE CHICAGO JOB!

~Kat

Don't miss the next story in
the Dragon Thief series!

THE POISONS BOOK JOB

Keep Reading for an excerpt!

The Poisons
Book Job

Excerpt

ONE

Myra slipped across the roofs of the Brownstones until coming to the roof she was aiming for. One that had a low wall and pressure sensors on the roof that were impossible to see if you didn't know they were there.

The Manhattan night kissed her cheeks with chilly air, the sounds of traffic over on Third a quiet hum. This neighborhood was exceptionally quiet at three in the morning, for Manhattan, but quiet in New York wasn't technically quiet. A couple of dogs barked a few streets over, which meant at least two people had to take their dogs out for walks at this time of night. She loved animals, but this is why, if she were to get a pet, it would be a cat. They could pee on their own while she was out working.

A cat burglar getting a cat might be clichéd, though.

The roof she needed to cross was wide and mostly empty, unlike the one she was standing in which was covered in raised stones boxes filled with plants and had a nice set of patio furniture and an outdoor grill. There were even trellises with ivy growing over them, though the ivy was mostly dead at the moment, given they were rolling into winter. The roof she stood on topped a Brownstone owned by a family that sent their two twin girls to private school and had parties up here that they claimed were for family but an awful lot of the mother's associates from the big accounting firm where she was a partner got invited.

Currently, the entire family was out of the country for a ski vacation, and the staff didn't spend the night. Which made this building a safe place to work from.

The roof Myra was aiming for was a wide-open square but for the small raised hut that led inside to the stairwell. The gray stone tiles on the roof looked ordinary and harmless. But her research confirmed they were sensitive enough to detect a pigeon landing on them. Which was probably annoying to the people who had to monitor the activity because there were a lot of pigeons in the city.

She pulled a hook and wire from a pocket of her jacket, and using a little spell to ensure the hook landed against the raised hut on the first throw, she swung and tossed the metal barbs, catching a sharp lip of the hut. She tied off the other end of the long wire to a metal loop fixed into the accountant's roof, a metal loop used to chain the grill down most of the time—for some reason, the residents hadn't bothered chaining the grill last time they'd used it. Maybe they'd assumed no one would try to steal it from off the roof?

There was an irony there since she was an actual thief but *wasn't* going to be stealing the grill. She had something a little different in mind.

She grabbed the wire, her gloved hands protecting her skin, and swung up so her legs hooked over, stretched out so she could use her feet to help her shimmy along the wire. Dangling over the motion sensor tiles, moving fast along the thin wire, she mentally asked all pigeons in the area to stay away for the next fifteen minutes.

The painting she was here for wasn't hanging on any of the walls inside the five story Brownstone. It wasn't kept inside a vault either, which was amusing to her. It was tilted against a wall in a closet on the third floor, one of many gently stacked into the closet, waiting for its rotation when it actually would get a position on a wall somewhere.

The Brownstone was owned, outwardly, by a small agency that claimed to represent artists in the city. Supposedly, all the art inside the mansion consisted of clients' work either given to the agency as a gift, or donated to the agency for resale. In point of fact, most of it was stolen from clients who were having trouble paying rent and buying groceries because their "agents" couldn't get them gallery showings or sell any of their work for more than a pittance.

Myra liked artists. It was a strange, but probably predictable thing, for a thief to have a soft spot for the people who created the things she stole. She never actually stole things from the artists, though. She stole things from the rich people who bought the artists' work.

Or in this case, stole the work first.

And this particular piece was worth a fortune according to an appraiser Myra sometimes worked with, but the agency had told the artist it was only worth a hundred dollars and they were being generous giving her that much. The artist was a single mother about to be evicted. Myra really didn't like that. So here she was, breaking and entering, not for her own amusement this time, but to help an artist out.

She might be a thief, but there were lines. And standards. And she had no compunctions about stealing from other thieves.

The hut was sturdy enough so that when she crawled on to it, it didn't even groan under her weight. Leaving the hook in place for her escape, she used the same lip that held the hook secure and folder herself over and down, hanging in front of the locked door without touching the tiles. Once she was certain her handhold wouldn't collapse, she released one hand and used a little spell to open the door. She could pick the lock in a pinch, but the spell finessed the lock in twenty seconds, saving her time.

Despite the pressure tiles all over the roof, the lock itself wasn't complicated. And the interior of the hut wasn't monitored or alarmed.

Sometimes thieves had blind spots. She liked to take advantage of those.

She slipped downstairs to the closet containing the piece she wanted, the house dark and quiet. No one actually lived here. This was a glorified warehouse and, when necessary, a fancy sort of office for the agency. The head of the agency, a man whose nasal voice irritated every last one of Myra's nerves, entertained wealthy clients here when he had something to sell, and intimidated eager artists here when he was trying to rope in a gullible aspirant.

When not in use, the place had a decent security system in place, but it was focused on entrance and exit points. Windows, doors, the roof. There was an elevator that was locked down when no one was using the house. And the first two floors had cameras in place that could be turned on remotely—and were during events so the agency's security team could monitor and spy on potential clients and customers.

But on the top three floors, the security was limited to doors and windows. A weird system, but it worked for her.

The lock on the storage closet was a cute little biosensor thing that didn't stand up to her spells and lock picks for more than thirty seconds. It tried, though. She was in and out of the closet in moments, waving her fingers over the locks to spell it sealed again.

Locked room mystery, she thought as she hurried back up to the roof.

The hardwood stairs didn't creak under her feet, but they might have if she hadn't had on her specialized shoes, a bit like ballet slippers that were almost like walking in socks, and had a little spell in the sole that helped dampen sound. She'd watched the building all day and knew it was empty, but better to be safe than sorry.

She tucked the painting into the small black nylon backpack she wore, which was just large enough to fit around the frameless one foot by one foot canvas, then opened the door onto the roof and reached up for the wire still taunt overhead.

She didn't scream when someone touched her gloved hand. But it was close. Years of training and practice keeping the surge of adrenaline spiked by irritated surprise from erupting out of her mouth. She looked up, prepared to run back into the house and escape through her alternate exit point.

Then cursed under her breath and shook her head, scowling up at the dragon shifter prince casually sitting on the hut above her.

Don't Miss Myra and Christopher's
next adventure in

THE POISONS BOOK JOB

Out now!

Join Kat's Newsletter

Stay Up-to-Date

On all Kat's News, Updates, and fun extras

New Subscriber Get Two Exclusive Stories Just for Signing up!

bit.ly/KatSimonsNewsletter

Paranormal Romance

From

KAT SIMONS

Books By Kat Simons

Dragon Thief Series

<u>Season One</u>

Dragon Thief

The Chicago Job

The Poisons Book Job

The Vault Job

The Femme Fatale Job

The Scavenger Job

<u>Season Two</u>

The Crown of Kingship Job

The Green Scroll Job

The Payback Job

Pick Your Genre Collections

Who Steals a Dragon

The Cary Redmond Series

* The Trouble Black Cats and Demons * The Trouble with Ghouls and Serial Killers * The Trouble with

Leopard Queens and Shifter Wars * The Trouble with Baby Gods and Vampires * The Trouble with Magic and Faery Curses * The Trouble with Wizards and Old Enemies * The Trouble with Death and Demon Gods

The Cary Redmond Series Box Set Books 1-3

Cary Redmond Short Stories

* When Cary Met Jaxer * When Cary Met Pickles * When Cary Met Marianne * When Cary Met Lucy * When Cary Met Angie * Cary and Deacon (Try to) Go on a Date * Date Night Take Two * Third Date's the Charm * Cary vs the Goblin King * Dinner with the Joneses * Cary and the Cursed Jack-O'-Lantern * Cary and the Demon Witch * Cary Goes to Hawaii * Cary Holidays * Cary and Dragons and Goblins * Cary's Galentine's Day * Cary at the Haunt and Howl * Cary's Leprechaun Troubles * Cary's Beltane Night Out *

When Cary Met the Good Guys (Collection 1)

Dates, Dinners, and Other Disasters (Collection 2)

Witches and Weavers and Ghosts, Oh Boy (Collection 3)

A Very Cary Holiday (Collection 4)

Romancing the Leopard: A Tiger Shifters-Cary Redmond Crossover Novel

Tiger Shifters Series

* Once Upon a Tiger * Along Came a Tiger * Here There Be Tigers * Her Tiger To Take * To Tempt a Tiger * Down Will Come Tiger * To Catch a Tiger * What a Tiger Wants * Taming Her Tiger

Tiger Shifters Series Vol 1 (Books 1 - 3)

Tiger Shifters Series Vol 2 (Books 4 - 6)

Seven Families Series

Wolf Family

Darkness in Stone

Redemption in Stone

Fated in Stone

Wolf in Stone: A Seven Families Box Set, Books 1-3

Demon Witch Series

Howling Dreadful

Moonlit Strange

Bone Lantern Witch

Spiderweb Witch

Storm Shadow Witch

Darkling Mist Witch

Joan of Kerry Series

Joan of Kerry: Joan and the Abhartach

Joan and the Leprechaun

Joan and the Kraken

Joan and the Selkie

Joan and the Goblins

Haunts and Howls Collections

Haunts and Howls and Guardian Spells

Haunts and Howls Where Demons Dwell

Haunts and Howls and Jesters Bells

*Tombstone Wizard * The Unshattered Sword *
Destiny Through the Cats Eyes * Going Out of
Business: Everything's for Sale * Anger Management *
Demonic Dates * Friday's Curious Shop * The Museum
of Small Art's Everyman * Burning Inside a Stone
Circle * Bored Questless * I Just Ate a Bug * Ting Ling
* Sophie Saves the World * Black Water Hawthorns
*To Dance in Fallow Fields at Midnight *

About the Author

Kat Simons earned her Ph.D. in animal behavior, working with animals as diverse as dolphins and deer. She brought her experience and knowledge of biology to her paranormal romance and urban fantasy fiction, where she delights in taking nature and turning it on its ear. She writes urban fantasy, contemporary fantasy, and paranormal romance in series which combine action adventure, the otherworldly, and a frequent dose of sexy romance.

The newest book in her bestselling romantic urban fantasy series about Protector Cary Redmond, The Trouble with Shifters and Fae Courts, sees a new direction for the intrepid Protector, her sexy leopard shifter mate, and the entire crew. Kat also launched a new novella length Paranormal Romance series that follows the adventures of a magical thief and the dragon shifter prince she just can't seem to shake—and really doesn't want to. The first season of the Dragon Thief series released throughout 2024.

Season Two begins in 2025 with The Crown of Kingship Job.

For something a little different, Kat also publishes fantasy, science fiction, and the occasional hockey romance under the name Isabo Kelly (https://www.isabokelly.com).

After traveling the world, living in places like Hawaii, Germany, and Ireland, Kat now lives in New York City with her family and a library's worth of books.

For more on Kat and her future books

Website: https://www.katsimons.com/
Newsletter: https://bit.ly/KatSimonsNewsletter

KatSimonsBooks

https://www.katsimonsbooks.com
https://www.TheCafeatKatSimonsBooks.com

Social Media

Facebook Page: https://www.facebook.com/
KatSimonsAuthor
BookBub: https://www.bookbub.com/authors/kat-simons
Bluesky: https://bsky.app/profile/katsimons.bsky.social
Instagram: https://www.instagram.com/isabokelly/
Threads: https://www.threads.net/@isabokelly